A VERY BOSSY CHRISTMAS

KAYLEY LORING

A Very BOSSY Christmas

Kayley Loring

COVER DESIGN: Kari March Designs
COVER PHOTO: © Maurizio Montani
http://www.mauriziomontani.it/
DEVELOPMENTAL EDITING: Jennifer Mirabelli
COPY EDITING: Jenny Rarden
PROOFREADING: Once Upon a Typo

FUNNY SEXY SWEET ROMANCE
Kayley
LORING
KAYLEY LORING

Happy holidays to you, dear reader.
May the new year be merry and bright
and not suck as hard as 2020 has,
because yeesh.

Chapter One

DECLAN: You at the office?
DECLAN: Cooper. You there?
DECLAN: Seriously, you need to respond. No matter where you are right now.
DECLAN: But you'd better be at the office.
MADDIE: Yes, Your Highness. I am at the office. Are you on your way in? Because I thought I felt the temperature drop a couple of degrees just now.
DECLAN: Haven't left home yet, but a lot of women display physical signs of a slight drop in temperature when I'm approaching, Cooper. It's adorable that you're so excited to see me.
MADDIE: Please refer to every eye roll I have ever executed in response to half of the things you say because I'm too busy organizing your life to find the emoji.
DECLAN: Set up a quick call for me with

Drucker before my meeting with Shapiro so he can update me on the Branson Residences deal. Just a phone call. I don't want him stopping by my office.
MADDIE: Yes sir.
DECLAN: Please refer to every eye roll I have ever executed every time you call me "sir." But also keep calling me sir.
MADDIE: Anything else I can do for you before you grace us with your presence, Mr. Cannavale?
DECLAN: Everything else, Cooper. And coffee served with a special holiday smile.
MADDIE: Fa la la la la la la la--be right back with your order, hon. <face with rolling eyes emoji>

TWO

Declan

FROSTY THE BOSSMAN

The drive up Madison Avenue is slower than usual this time of the morning, but it's satisfying to lean on the horn when some asshole in an Impala tries to cut in front of me. I flip the driver off as I pass him, and he does it right back, but he looks confused when he sees me. He's clearly not a tourist, so I don't know what's confusing about a driver giving another driver the finger in Manhattan. Then I catch a glimpse of my reflection in the rearview mirror and realize I'm smiling.

I have a big dumb grin on my face.

For no reason.

No reason other than I'm on my way to work and I love my job.

Okay, I *like* my job.

But I love to work.

And I like to work with people who can actually keep up with me.

Okay, I love it.

It's rare.

It's almost as satisfying as leaning on the horn when some asshole tries to cut in front of me.

It's a lot more satisfying than watching women cry after I've calmly explained to them exactly what they've done wrong and questioning their ability to perform the most mundane tasks.

Not that I enjoy making women cry.

I hate making women cry.

Especially when they should be answering my phone and redoing whatever mundane task I've asked them to perform.

But I don't have to do that anymore.

Because Maddie Cooper is competent.

Maddie Cooper can handle me.

Maddie Cooper can give as good as she gets.

Maddie Cooper is hot and claims to hate me.

It's problematic.

But she's one problem I'm not willing to solve.

Not yet, anyway.

And just like that, I'm frowning again.

You happy now, Impala?

Yeah. This feels right. This feels like my fucking life this year.

I lean on the horn again because *fuck you, everyone in front of me.*

I'm about to call Cooper, just as my sister's name

and number come up. She's not supposed to try me on my work phone unless it's an emergency.

Shit. Now what?

"Casey?"

"Are you coming for Christmas or not?"

"Seriously? That's why you're calling me on my work phone? During business hours?"

"Also to say good morning, asshole."

"Good morning, asshat, and *not.* But don't tell Ma—I haven't called her yet."

"I knew it. Declan..."

"I have to work."

"I thought you started in-house lawyering so you could have a better quality of life."

"I did. And I have a much better view from my office now."

That is true in ways that I will not be explaining to my sister.

"Dec. Don't be glib."

"I'm not being glib. I only work fifty-five hours a week, and I get six hours of sleep a night on weekends. I'm practically a slacker. I can't help it if New York honesty sounds like superficial insincerity to people in Ohio. And what makes you think the quality of my life would improve if I went home for Christmas this year? I'm dying to see most of you, but I can't. It's not like it would be easy for me either way…"

Boom. There it is. Saying things without saying things and attempting to elicit sympathy. It's the only way I've been able to talk to the women in my personal life since I was five years old.

My sister sighs, loudly, because she carries the weight of the entire Cannavale family on her shoulders. Most of us are men, and we're composed of lean muscle, my father's relentless pride, my mother's ability to talk anyone into or out of anything, Irish whiskey, and my nonna's meatballs and deep-fried-everything that takes half a year to digest. We're heavy. We're belligerent. And we all want our ma and sister to love us the best.

Casey is the only girl of five kids, and she's been the peacemaker since the day she was born. It's a shit job, and none of us assholes are gonna do it.

"I hate this," she offers, her tone softening. "Have you talked to either of them?"

"No and it wouldn't change anything if I did."

"Dec..."

"Is *that* why you called? Because if it is—"

"It's not—I just want to see you. We all do. You know how I feel about what's going on..."

Yessssss. I'm still her favorite brother.

"I do, Case. And I appreciate it. And I've told you it's not necessary for you to feel anything about it. Because I'm fine. It is what it is. I'm just busy with work and I can't make it home. All there is to it."

"Not even for dinner on Christmas Eve?"

"I can't leave town—there's a lot going on. I'm working straight through the holidays."

"How can they make you do that?"

"Nobody's *making* me do it. I'm the general counsel. Of one of the top real estate firms in the city. We have nine offices—none of them will be closed over the holidays, and it's my job to oversee all legal matters."

This is technically true. Our offices won't be closed. Which is why I'll be there working and so will my assistant. But I don't *have* to be there working straight through the holidays. I want to. *And fuck you, Catholic guilt. That's enough out of you.*

"Yeah yeah yeah, Mr. Bigshot Lawyer in the City That Never Sleeps. I get it. It sucks. But I get it."

"It does suck."

"But you're coming to..." She doesn't even finish that sentence, and I don't need to hear the rest of it.

"Yeah. I'm not gonna miss it. But I'll be in and out. Quick trip. How's my favorite Jedi doing?" I change the subject fast.

"Your attempts at buying her love have paid off big-time. The presents you sent don't even fit under the tree—you're making the rest of us look bad."

"So what else is new? That's been a thing ever since I had a face."

She laughs, but she can't argue with that because it's a fact. "You really can't fly in just for dinner? You could fly back to New York that night, right? You could handle it for a few hours. Come on."

I couldn't. That's the God's honest truth. I couldn't handle it, and I don't want one person on earth to know this.

"I can handle it—I just don't want to, and I can't take even half a day off."

"Fine. I understand."

"Good."

She exhales for so long it worries me. That can't be good for her brain. Finally, she takes a deep breath and says very calmly, "I'm telling Ma."

"Do *not* tell Ma—Casey!"

"Good luck explaining to *her* why you're not coming!"

I slap the top of the dashboard. She's older than me, but I hate it when she doesn't listen.

"I will tell her myself… Case? Casey..."

She hung up on me.

That is not good.

This will not be good for me.

There's a ninety percent chance that it was just a threat, but I am one hundred percent fucked if I don't talk to my ma sooner rather than later.

If I call, I'll need a plan, and I don't have one yet.

If my ma calls, I can avoid her for about six hours, tops. Any longer than that, and I'm the least favorite son for months. She won't be on my side, and I *need* the women on my side.

This is bad.

I finally realize there's an old lady in the middle of the crosswalk and she's flipping me the double bird. Only, you can hardly tell that her middle fingers are up because she's wearing men's gloves that are too big for her. I realize I'm leaning on the horn. And the old lady is using a walker.

This is really bad.

I raise my hands in the air in surrender, mouthing

I am so sorry—it was an accident! And then clasp my hands together, begging for forgiveness.

That's when someone else tosses their coffee at my car and yells "Eat a bag of dicks, you old Grinch!" Now all the cars behind me are honking because the light has changed and the old lady is still in the middle of the crosswalk, giving me the stink eye.

Old? Since when is thirty-two old? Who does that little shit think he's talking to?

He doesn't even help the old lady across the street. I want to get out of my car and do it, but she'd probably think I'm just trying to make her move faster. Which would be mostly true.

It's not even eight o'clock yet, and I already hate this day.

Work.

I just need a few hours at the office, and then I'll feel good and I'll know my place in the world again.

Because I love my work.

Sentinel is the tenth-largest real estate firm in New York City in terms of dollar volume of listings. The properties are luxury. The offices are shiny but not as shiny as the law firm I left seven months ago. Everyone here works hard but not as hard as everyone works in Big Law. This is New York, so looking good matters, but these people aren't too slick because no one's the star of a reality show. Okay, maybe I'm a little slick, but only because it's impossible to tone down my alarming good looks and impeccable style. And it's real estate, so everyone is personable—but not as personable as your friendly neighborhood real estate agent in Ohio. Because this is New York. So I don't have to deal with a bunch of friendly brokers all up in my face every day. They let me do my job, and I'm more than happy to let them do theirs as long as they don't fuck things up by being idiots or doing anything illegal.

I did start in-house lawyering here so I could have a better quality of life. It's true.

That's why I'm the general counsel at Sentinel, as opposed to one of the top three firms.

A little less income than Big Law, sure, but also less stress and hours.

It was time for me to get a life.

It was time for me to prove—to no one in particular—that I could make room for another person in that spacious new life.

I just didn't expect to realize exactly how empty my life had become as soon as I'd made the change.

Fortunately, I don't have time to dwell on that kind of thing anymore.

Fortunately, my work life is fulfilling in a way that it has never been before.

I could do with a lot less of the Christmas decorations and holiday cheer around the corporate office, though.

As soon as I step off the elevator and into the Sentinel lobby, I'm greeted by Cindy the unbearably happy receptionist. Which is weird because she started to back off after I'd been here for about a week. That made me like her more.

"Happy holidays, Mr. Cannavale!"

"Nope."

"I'm so happy you'll be at the holiday party next week!"

"I won't be there."

"Oh really? Because Maddie just RSVP'd yes for you. We got the deluxe karaoke machine this year, so it should be extra fun."

"Oh *really?* Maddie RSVP'd 'yes' to the office party, you say?"

"Yeah, like ten minutes ago."

Interesting.

Unexpected.

Absolutely unacceptable.

But hot.

And there she is. The woman who keeps my schedule running smoothly and handles me with the sleek, unruffled grace of a highly skilled assassin. She shields me from all of the assholes and idiots I don't want to deal with. I like it. She's the executive assistant of my dreams and the succubus from my filthiest, most confusing adolescent nightmares. She's the woman who's kept me in a constant state of blue balls for the past two months. Today, she's torturing me with a tight black pencil skirt, knee-high boots, and a cashmere sweater that looks like it was spray painted onto her evil curves. Her brown hair is so shiny; I believe her shampoo is made from the semen of demonic stallions. It's up in a bun, revealing the satiny smooth skin of her long neck. I could spend an hour or twelve just kissing that neck, and I bet she'd like it too.

But that's neither here nor there.

She's standing by her desk with a coffee mug in one hand, her other hand resting just above her hip, right where I should be gripping her.

"Cooper."

"Morning, Sunshine. You've got your conference call with Drucker in ten minutes, and Harvey from Cravath had to push your lunch to the new year because he's an actual human who takes time off to be with his family during the holidays."

"I'm not going to the office party next week."

"I'm pretty sure you are. Let me just check your schedule. Hang on…" She mimes looking at a schedule on a monitor. "Yup. December 22nd, five to five thirty or later, office holiday party."

She follows me into my office, shutting the glass door behind her. Those glass walls and doors were my least favorite thing about this office until two months ago.

"Get it off my schedule."

"I know it may feel like I RSVP'd 'yes' in order to punish you, and I'm glad it feels like punishment, but the entire executive team will be in attendance. So I'm actually doing my job and helping you to look like slightly less of a terrible person."

She places the coffee mug on my desk, on the coaster, leaning forward and exposing just enough bra and cleavage to make a grown man cry. She turns the mug around so the ***World's Best Boss*** text is facing me and winks. I fucking love it when she winks at me. Even when she's being a sassy little turd.

I take a seat and glower at her. "You're telling me Shapiro is going to this thing?"

"Yes, the founder and CEO of this company will be attending the festivities along with most of the employees from all of the offices. Including his beloved General Counsel."

Both hands rest on her hips now, and she sticks her chest out, defiant and hot. Hot and defiant and endlessly problematic. But really hot.

"That is very disappointing. Will you be there? If I have to go, then you do too."

"Why yes. I and the rest of the executive assistants as well as the entire support staff will be there—thanks for asking!"

"Who's going to answer the phones? Or are we all hoping to drop off the list of top ten New York real estate firms next year?"

"They're bringing in temps to cover the phones that day."

"Thought of everything, huh?"

"Yeah, and I hear they got the deluxe karaoke machine, so…" She smirks at me. That smirk does things to me. That smirk is highly problematic.

"Tell one of the interns to get my car washed."

"Right away, sir." She bats her eyelashes.

"But not the one who did it the last time—he's a smoker. And not the girl who did it the time before that—my car was infused with her perfume for a week, and I did not like it."

"I'll be sure to request the one who always gets onion rings at White Castle on his way to the car wash."

I raise the coffee mug to sniff it. "What is this?"

"A steaming hot cup of the tears of your former assistants."

"That's funny, because it smells like pumpkin spice."

"That's hilarious, because it's a pumpkin spice latte."

"That's interesting because I only drink black coffee and espresso. You know that."

"I thought maybe the pumpkin spice would put you in the holiday spirit."

"Fuck holiday spirit. Fuck pumpkin spice."

She crosses her arms in front of her ample, problematic chest. "Maybe you should. It would probably put you in a better mood…"

I narrow my eyes at her. "Are you trying to get yourself fired, Cooper?"

"Yes, but I'm not expecting a Christmas miracle."

I hand her back the coffee cup. "Please accept this pumpkin spice latte in lieu of said miracle."

"Blech, no thank you. I hate flavored coffee. Unless it's, y'know, *grown-up* coffee."

Every now and then I detect the slightest hint of Staten Island in the way she talks, and it makes whatever she's saying sound dirty. And I like it.

She takes a sip of the latte, grimacing. "Blech. Horrible."

It's fucking adorable when she wrinkles her nose like that. "Why'd you take a sip if you hate flavored coffee?"

"I thought maybe I'd like this one."

"Serves you right for being an optimist. I need the contracts for the Branson deal in front of me."

"Emailed them to you five minutes ago. Would you like me to purchase a Secret Santa gift on your behalf? I'm leaving early this afternoon to take my niece shopping—I can pick something up for you."

I pull up the email on my computer. She added a winking face emoji to the subject line. "Not necessary."

"You have to participate, or it isn't fair to whichever unfortunate soul whose name you drew."

"I *am* participating. For your information, I happen to be a world-class gift giver. I will be purchasing it myself."

I scan the documents and make a couple of notes, but it seems she's still standing there, staring down at me.

"Anything else?"

"Once again, I would like to request the 25th off so I can spend it with my family."

I get an email notification on my personal phone and glance down at it while she's telling me that none of the other executives or their assistants are working from the 23rd until the 28th.

"Once again, I must remind you that you will be

earning premium holiday pay."

The email is from my brother Brady. I delete it without reading it. This means my sister called him right after she called me. That means a call from my mother is imminent. That means I'm going to have to lie to my ma. That means instead of feeling sorry for myself, I'll hate myself.

"I don't care about making overtime on Christmas," she continues. "I want to see my sister's baby and hang out with my family."

I vigorously scrub my face with the palms of my hands, grunting.

"You can see them for dinner. It's not my fault we're so busy, and it's definitely not my fault Christmas is on a weekday."

"It's on a Friday."

"Friday is a weekday, Cooper. Would you like to try to convince me otherwise, or would you like to let me finish reading through this contract before Drucker calls?"

She mumbles something about my moods and me being the devil while turning on her four-inch heels and giving me a fantastic view of her perfect round ass in that tight black skirt. I watch that ass sway all the way out of my office. I keep watching her through the glass wall between us as she takes a seat at her desk, blowing air out of her big puffy lips and cursing me under her breath.

I wish she were whispering those angry filthy curses into my ear, but my day has still gotten so much better already.

THREE

Maddie

FROSTY, YOU BLOW, MAN

In the grand scheme of things, being subjected to the moods and demands of a horrifically gorgeous man in a beautiful suit isn't the worst thing anyone ever had to deal with. But Declan Cannavale can bite me. He can kiss my butt and he can blow me and he can go take a long walk off a short, icy pier. I might have to strip his beautiful suit off and lick him from head to toe first before marching him out into the freezing-cold December air. But only because I'd want him to suffer more.

Not because I'm dying to lick all six-foot-two-inches of his stupidly amazing body from head to toe.

Because I'm not.

It's not like I can't handle working for him. I mean, I'd rather handle him firmly around his neck. But I know how to deal with these guys who think they can get away with anything just because they're lickable.

Still, if I could go back to working for Artie, I would.

In a heartbeat.

I had worked for Artie ever since I graduated from college. He's old and sweet and never gave me a single moment of grief. I would have worked for him forever. But no matter how much I beg and plead with him, he refuses to come out of retirement just so I can quit this ridiculous well-paid job.

I remember when Declan's office would call Artie, back when Declan worked in Big Law. I'd listen in. Declan even dialed the phone himself every now and then and we'd chat. He was fine back then. Apparently, when he'd heard that Artie was going to retire, he told him he wanted to hire me ASAP.

Artie vouched for him. Said he was "a class act with a heart of gold." Told me he really hoped I'd take this job instead of the one for the partner at the law firm because I'd have better work-life balance. You know what I got? A grumpy boss with a heart of coal. Fifty-five-hour work weeks. Texts and emails every night and all weekend. So many eye-roll–inducing one-liners that I'm afraid my eyeballs might get stuck in the back of my head one of these days. A chronically clenched jaw and a nonstop angry lady boner. My teeth are being ground to a fine dust, and the head of my Hitachi Magic Wand now has a dent in it.

"Aunt Maddie, why are you stabbing at your keyboard like that?"

"What? Oh…" My niece has been sitting beside me so quietly, I completely forgot she was there.

Piper. She's thirteen and adorable. My sister has been so busy with the new baby, and Piper's been all bummed out because she's the only girl in eighth grade who doesn't have boobs yet. So I offered to take her Christmas shopping, but for some reason she couldn't wait until the weekend.

She closes the textbook she's been reading, carefully using her highlighter pen as a bookmark, and asks, "When can we go shopping?"

"I just have to wait until my boss gets back from his meeting in a minute, and then we're outta here. That okay?"

"Okay." She nudges her glasses up the bridge of her nose as she opens her book again. "Should I hide or something? I don't want him to be mean to me."

"He won't be mean to you, honey… Probably… I hope." I will knee him in the balls if he's mean to my niece.

"Well hello there," says an all too familiar voice in a very unfamiliar tone. "Are you training a new assistant for me, Cooper? Because I also happen to be a highlighter person. This could work out very well."

I look away from my monitor and find Declan smiling at Piper. Smiling with his supernatural amber eyes. Like an actual human. I can see his teeth, and there is a heretofore unseen dimple in his left cheek.

I don't understand what's happening.

"Cooper?" He stares down at me quizzically. "You okay?"

"Are *you* okay? What's happening to your face?"

"It's smiling, Coop." He knows I hate it when he calls me "Coop." He holds his laptop to his chest and gives Piper a cool little wave. "Hi, I'm Declan," he says to her. "And you are?"

"Piper. Hey."

"Hey."

"Um. This is my niece. Piper, this is my boss, Mr. Cannavale. How was your meeting?"

"It was not terrible. Can you get Victor on the phone for me? And ask what's-his-name's assistant for the by-laws for the—"

"She just emailed them to you. I'll get Victor, and then Holly will be covering my desk for the rest of the day so I can take my adorable niece shopping."

"Oh great. Sounds fun." He winks at Piper and then flashes me with the kind of smile that makes me check his hands to make sure there aren't any knives in them. Because he looks all kinds of stabby. "Can I talk to you in my office for a second?"

Eye roll.

"I'll be right back, Piper. Why don't you start packing up your bag so we can go."

I follow Declan into his office and shut the door behind myself.

He drops his laptop onto the leather sofa and turns back to face me with a wide stance, his arms crossed at his chest. "You're going shopping? At five o'clock? Today?"

"I told you this morning and yesterday evening and two days ago. As I just said, Holly the floater will be covering for me."

"How long were you planning on shopping for?"

"She's Christmas shopping for her friends and parents. It'll take a couple of hours, at least."

"But you're coming back afterwards, right?"

"To the office?"

"Yes, Cooper. To the office. Where you work. For me."

That's it. My arms are crossed in front of my chest now too. "You're asking me if I'm coming back to the office after seven tonight?"

He shrugs. "I'll still be here."

"And Holly will stay until you leave."

"Who?"

"Holly. The floater."

"What's a floater?"

"Someone whose job it is to cover an assistant's desk when said assistant is unable to cover it herself."

"For instance, when said assistant is shopping with a family member in the middle of a workday?"

"Five pm is hardly the middle of the workday, and you know what—I have made the proper arrangements for you. My niece rode the subway on her own from the Upper West Side, and now I am going to get Victor on the phone for you and then I am going to take my niece Christmas shopping." I turn on my heels for like the ninth time today and walk away from him before he tells me to come back after dinner.

I can feel him glaring at my back. Or possibly

slightly lower than my back. I leave the door open, but he doesn't say anything else. Except when he calls out to Piper to tell her to have fun shopping. Which is so annoying.

Piper is just a silent pulsating heart-eyes emoji face all the way until we exit the building onto Madison Avenue, when she finally exclaims, "*Sheeeww.* Your boss's butt is perfect!"

"Piper! Shhh!" It's so cold, I can see our breath.

"It is! Have you looked at it?"

"No. He's my boss. Come on, Fifth Avenue is this way."

"You should check it out. It's perfect."

"I doubt it. Should we go to H&M first?"

"You're right. It's too flat."

"It's not flat!"

"Aha! You *have* looked at it!"

"Only when it was unavoidable. Stop talking about my boss's butt."

"But it's the best one I've ever seen IRL."

"Don't say IRL. Say *in real life* when you're not texting."

"WTF are you so grumpy and bossy RN?"

"Piper, I'm not the grumpy, bossy one. Declan is. Do you want to grab something to eat first or after we shop a little?" Now I'm just mad at him for being nice to my niece. And for having such a hot butt. What a dick move.

"He's a hottie with a body. He must do squats all day long."

"Oh my God—why don't you watch a Shawn Mendes video on your phone or something to wipe my boss from your memory."

"Shawn Mendes seems so young to me now. I want to look at grown-man abs. Have you seen Declan with his shirt off? I bet he has abs."

"Everyone has abs."

"I want to see Declan's abs."

"Stop calling him Declan."

"But he told me to."

"We don't *all* have to do what he tells us to do. At least I'm paid to do it. And even then, I don't do everything he tells me to do—because he's not right about everything."

"You seem to care an awful lot about him."

"No I don't."

"I would do literally anything he told me to do. I would lick him like a candy cane."

"Piper."

"Just sayin'."

"You have no idea what you're sayin'. Seriously, you have to stop saying things like that. Have you ever kissed a boy?"

"Yes. In spin the bottle at Shoshana's b-day party last month. I bumped noses with Drake G, so our lips didn't really touch, but I still count it as kissing."

"Piper, you shouldn't talk about licking boys, and you really shouldn't talk about licking men."

"Okay. I definitely think *you* should lick him, though."

"You definitely shouldn't talk about me licking my boss—I would never." I might think about it, but I would *never.* In real life, I'd rather lick eggnog off the bottom of my boots than lick Declan Cannavale. And I *hate* eggnog.

Speak of licking the devil, and the work phone in your pocket vibrates…

DECLAN: COOPER. COME BACK.

"Oh for shit's sake."

"Is it Declan?"

"Yes. I haven't even been gone for two minutes, and already he's texting me."

"Lucky. No boys ever text me."

"Enjoy it while it lasts."

Chapter Four

DECLAN: What is the name of that terrible woman at your desk?
MADDIE: That's Holly. The floater. Be nice to her!!!
DECLAN: She's always smiling at me. It's creepy.
MADDIE: She's a really nice person who is good at her job.
DECLAN: When are you coming back?
MADDIE: I literally just left.
DECLAN: That is not an answer.
MADDIE: I thought I made it clear that I'm not coming back to the office tonight.
DECLAN: Unacceptable.
MADDIE: What exactly do you need me to do tonight that can't be done by Holly?
DECLAN: I need you to sit at that desk and not smile at me like a creep.
MADDIE: Trust me, that is exactly what I'll

be doing tomorrow and for the rest of my unbearable tenure as your assistant. Anything else?
MADDIE: Anything? Else? Speak now or forever hold your peace.
MADDIE: For tonight, anyway. Like I said, I'm not expecting any Christmas miracles.
DECLAN: Everything else, Cooper. Everything else. Good night.

🎄

DECLAN: Cooper? You there? One more question.
MADDIE: Always here for you, Declan! <heart eyes emoji>
DECLAN: Well now, that's more like it.
MADDIE: You should totally come meet us for dinner at Panera after we go to Best Buy LOL <dancing lady emoji> <dancing lady emoji> <dancing lady emoji>
DECLAN: Are you drunk right now?
MADDIE: Would you like me to be? <winking face emoji>
DECLAN: Kind of. What's the name of the new guy at the mayor's office? The younger one with the beard? I don't know how to ask the floater to get him on the phone for me.
MADDIE: Um. Zac?
DECLAN: He looks nothing like Zac Efron.
MADDIE: Jake?

DECLAN: Hilarious. Are you going to list all of the actors with beards? Because I actually have to call him now-ish.
MADDIE: Declan. That was my niece. I was in the dressing room. His name is Tom Linklater.
DECLAN: She's hired.
MADDIE: OMG I will totally work for you!!! LOL. You don't even have to pay me lolol.
MADDIE: Sorry, I had to pay for something and she grabbed my phone. Let's not add child labor law violations to the list of terrible things you're capable of, Mr. Cannavale. I'm putting my phone away now. Have a good night.
DECLAN: There are exactly zero things on that list, FYI.
DECLAN: You don't get to have the last word, Cooper.
DECLAN: Cooper.
DECLAN: Fine, I have to call Tom Linklater anyway. Have a very merry dinner at Panera.

FIVE

Declan

MAMA'S BOY TO THE WORLD

Fuck the holidays. Fuck family dinners. And fuck my life.

My mother's voice mail has been burning a hole through my phone and my cold dead heart since six o'clock. It is now ten-thirty here and in Ohio. She'll still be up. If I wait until after midnight to call and leave a message, she'll know I was trying to avoid her. If I send her a text saying that I'll call her in the morning, she'll call me back immediately. If I don't answer, she will not stop calling. She. Will. Never. Stop. If I don't respond at all, I'm a dick. I literally have a degree in knowing whether or not I'm going to win an argument or not, and I am one hundred percent going down in flames with this one.

I don't even know what I'm going to say at this point, so I just have to nut up, make the call, and get this terrible part of my life over with.

Two more fingers of whiskey, and I take the plunge. I open up the cutlery drawer so I can have a fork ready—for when I'll have to stab myself in the thigh with it. For soul-crushing Catholic guilt reasons.

She answers before I even hear it ring. "Declan Sullivan Cannavale. You don't join us for Thanksgiving, and now you're avoiding us at Christmas too?"

"I'm not avoiding you, Ma. I'm busy. Hi."

"You're prioritizing work over family. Again. Hi. You sound hungry—did you eat dinner?"

"Yes. I had a steak."

"Oh Mr. Fancypants Magee over there with his steaks and his penthouse and his gallivantin' around town and his big important meetings that are more important to him than his own mother." I can hear her grinning. Mary Margaret O'Sullivan Cannavale is a first-generation Irish-American from Boston with a first class Irish Mammy personality. Sometimes she wields it like an adorable five-year-old with a toy lightsaber. Sometimes she uses it like a shiv in an impromptu street fight. She's going easy on me up front, but that just means she'll escalate if I don't head her off at the pass.

I scoff quietly. "I'm definitely not gallivanting around town."

"Oh yeah? Why's that? Sleeping at the office again?"

"Nope. I didn't want to say anything yet…but I've been seeing someone."

What the fuck, mouth?!

She's silent for a beat before saying, "Say that again so I know I didn't dream it."

"I've been seeing someone. I didn't want to say anything because of what's going on, but—"

"*'What's going on?'* What's going on is you've been breaking my heart letting me think you're all alone over there working all the time in that soulless crap hole. Now you're telling me you've got a girlfriend and you're keeping it a secret? From *me*?"

"It's not a secret. I just wasn't telling anyone yet. You know. Until I knew if it was serious or not."

Fuck you, mouth.

"So, what you're telling me is it's serious?"

Fuck me.

"It's still new" is what I'm saying at the same time that she says, "Bring her! Bring her to Christmas Eve dinner. *I'll* tell you if it's serious or not. It's settled."

"I don't know if—"

"Oh…" She lowers her voice. "Does she not celebrate Christmas?" Because this would be terrible, and she doesn't want my dad or the Virgin Mary to hear my answer.

"She celebrates Christmas." I pause for her audible sigh of relief. "I just have to see about her schedule. She works as much as I do. Almost exactly as much, actually…"

"Is she there with you now?"

"No. No, she's at her place. She took her niece shopping today."

Fuck you, brain.

I toss the fork back into the drawer because this conversation is all the torture and punishment I need.

"Ohhhh... She's good with kids! I like the sound of that."

"Ma."

"You know I always said you'd make a good father."

"It is definitely too soon to be thinking about that."

"I've been thinking about it ever since Eddie was born. The way you looked after him. Six years old and always looking out for the new baby. How much longer are you going to make me wait to become a grandmother? I'm not exactly getting any younger over here."

"You already have grandkids."

"I won't be happy until *all* of my babies are blessed with babies of their own—you know that."

"How is Eddie doing, anyway? I haven't heard from him in a while."

Thank God for Eddie. I can always bring him up when I need to shift the topic of conversation from what's missing in my life to the dumpster fire that is his love life. Take *that,* youngest son.

"Eddie's doing great, it sounds like."

"He is?"

Fuck you, Eddie.

"Sounds like he's finally met a nice girl, but *he* won't give me any details either."

"Ahh. Sounds about right."

"Don't try to change the subject, Mr. Esquire. You

bring this girlfriend of yours—what did you say her name was?"

"I didn't. It's Maddie." *Fuck you, Christmas.*

"Maddie! Now that's a charming name. She sounds Irish—love her already."

"Oh, she's a charmer, all right. But I'm not sure if she's got any Irish in her." *I'd like to put some Irish-Italian in her though.*

"Not sure? How could you not know something like that?" She sounds genuinely hurt that I'm not actively seeking out Irish-American women who are exactly like her.

"We've just had a lot of other things to talk about." *Like work. And how much she hates working for me. And how much she despises me as a person.*

"Well, I can't wait to meet her. Hang on." I can hear my dad's deep, muffled voice in the background. "It's Declan!" she yells out. "He's got a new girlfriend named Maddie! He's bringing her to the dinner. What? Turn down the TV I can't hear you! Stop yelling at me! Ugh—that man. Driving me nuts."

"I'll let you go if you need to—"

"Don't you hang up on me, Mister Bigshot. You'll bring Maddie on Christmas Eve. And you'll take her to Boston for the O'Sullivan gathering on the 22nd. You got the invitation."

I deleted the invitation.

"I don't think they invited me..."

"I saw they cc'd you, so don't try to get out of it. You're going. Granny and Grandad can't come for Christmas because of his foot. He has to keep it elevated as much as possible, so they can't travel now. Hopefully, by the wedding."

"Uh-huh."

"God knows I'd fly to Boston in a heartbeat, but I gotta stick around here every damn day to make sure your father doesn't accidentally burn the house down. Someone from my family's gotta be there, and you're the closest. They'll be so happy to see you with someone new."

"It only takes ten minutes longer to fly there from Cleveland. Why can't Aiden go?"

"Aiden's got kids."

"Right. And he can't afford to get alcohol poisoning from hanging out with the Irish side for a few hours."

"It's the truth."

"I can't just fly to Boston for a cocktail party."

"Oh yes, you can. You went for that meeting once —you think I don't remember?"

"That was for work."

"Uh-huh. I see how it is. *Enh.* It's fine. They'll both be dead soon anyway, so what's the point of spending time with them? They're just your mother's parents. My entire side of the family will be dead soon, probably from their livers giving out, so who gives a flyin' whatever, right?"

"Ma. I can't. I'm sorry, but I can't go to that. But I will bring her to Christmas Eve, all right? I promise."

She sighs. "Okay." She never really expected me to go to Boston. I know that tactic. She knows I know that tactic. "That's my good boy. And you'll bring her to…"

"Yeah, I'll bring her."

"I'll tell them. You don't have to—I'll tell everyone for you."

"Thanks, Ma. I appreciate it."

"Anything for my sweet boy…Hang on—*what?!*" My mother never pulls the phone away from her mouth when she yells at my dad. Ever. "It's in the cupboard! Not that one—the other one! *Yeah it is*—behind the thing! Don't you move my things around! Tony! Tony?! That man, I swear. I just want you to marry a nice woman who's as tolerant as I am, Dec. *Christ on a cracker.* I'll call you back."

"I actually have to call Maddie now, so…"

"Awww, you do that. I'm so excited to see you—I love you, my sweet, sweet boy."

"Love you."

Conversation over.

Now what?

Ma always said I'd catch my death from the cold if I went outside barefoot… I could try that. I could ask one of the women I was "gallivantin' around town" with earlier this year if they want to pretend to be named Maddie for a few nights, but I haven't seen any of them for a couple of months, and who needs *that* conversation?

Or I could just wait until I tell Cooper what I need her to assist me with over the holidays and wait for her to kill me slowly with eye rolls and sarcasm.

For the first time in two months, I *don't* reach for

my phone to text her when it seems like nothing else can save me.

But it seems that nothing—not even a phone call with my mother—can stop me from wondering if Maddie Cooper is naked right now.

Fuck my cold, dead heart.

SIX

Maddie

HERE COMES THE SANTA CLAUSE

It turns out the only thing more aggravating than dealing with a gorgeous, moody, demanding boss is experiencing said gorgeous moody boss when he appears to be making an effort to be courteous, tolerable, and somewhat pleasant.

The last two days at work were weird. Creepy. Ominous.

Like the scenes toward the end of a scary movie, where you're supposed to think that the axe murderer is dead and gone—so the heroine is walking around her kitchen barefoot, listening to a Van Morrison song, talking on the phone, and telling her friend not to worry about her anymore. Then pouring herself a glass of wine and getting into the shower. The camera slowly pans over to the basement door that she forgot to lock. The movie lulls you into a false sense of complacency right before shit gets real.

I never fall for it.

I never walk around my kitchen barefoot.

I always keep every door and window locked.

And I will not be lulled into a false sense of complacency with Declan Cannavale.

I'm suspicious. He's probably going to ask me to work through the night on Christmas Eve and Christmas Day or something. I won't do it. I don't care how good he smells. He stinks as a boss.

He didn't make me stay late last night. He hasn't texted me yet today, so I actually got to have a Saturday morning all to myself for the first time since I'd started working for him. And it's been great. I slept in. I drank hot cocoa in front of my Christmas tree while listening to "Ave Maria." *Okay, I drank hot chocolate with peppermint Schnapps at ten-thirty in the morning while listening to Mariah Carey.* I bought groceries. I'm able to walk down the sidewalk without bumping into people because I'm not busy responding to his texts.

And I don't miss him one little bit.

I'm just enjoying freezing my tits off on this beautiful arctic day in the East Village. My landlady, Mrs. Pavlovsky, is out sweeping the stoop of our building, as she does every day of the year. The trees are bare, and there's no snow or wind or even a speck of dust on the steps, but she likes to keep busy. And I love talking to her. This part of town is called Ukrainian Village, so it's not uncommon to hear her accent in this neighborhood. But I've missed chatting with her on weekends, because she's comforting to me in the way that her borscht is. She's weird and colorful and nourishing.

"Mrs. Pavlovsky, you aren't dressed warm enough," I tease. She's always telling me to put more clothes on, and now she's wearing an old, worn-out wool coat, even though she owns a freaking building in Manhattan.

"Pah!" She waves her hand dismissively. "*Zis* is nothing. Here—no wind. In Ukraine—cold to my bones. Here—cold only skin deep. Meh."

I wonder if my boss is only cold skin-deep. Maybe it just took him two months to warm up to me. Is that what's happening?

"Oooohhh. *Vat's zis* smile for, Magdalena? A man?" She calls me Magdalena, and she is about as good at pronouncing "w" and "th" sounds as I am at choosing boyfriends.

I wipe the smile from my face, walk up the steps, and open the front door to our building. "No smile. No man."

She follows me inside. "*Vy* you don't have man, Magdalena? Huh? *Vy?* You get man to go out on street *vis*, and I am not having to *vorry* no more. But now my heart is ache for you, *alvays*! *Nyet.* No good."

She has asked me to "help learn better to speak *ze* English," so I correct her. "You mean why don't I have a man to go out with?"

"Yes." She makes a great effort and manages to say, "Whyyyyy you don't have man? Not all man is like one *vis*...with...long hair, *alvays* crying."

The needy musician.

"Or man *vis* bags of avocado, *always* yelling about plastic."

The angry vegan environmentalist.

"Some man is *vonderful*. Like my Vladimir."

Her husband really was wonderful.

I pause by her front door and wait for her to unlock it. "You really don't have to worry about me. I've got my hands full with work right now."

"Pah! You know what your hands should be full of on weekend. Come. I have borscht and sausage for you. Come."

"I'm really fine," I protest. "I just bought groceries —but thank you."

"You let me put more fat on bones, and good man *vill* come for you. You *vill* see I'm right."

Twenty minutes later, I'm in my kitchen, biting into Mrs. Pavlovsky's reheated sausage and definitely not thinking about anyone else's sausage when my phone vibrates, and my heart starts racing. Because I'm hoping it's *not* Declan. And it's definitely not a sigh of disappointment when I see that it's my sister calling me. It's a sigh of relief. Because my sister Bex is my best friend and exactly the kind of person I should be talking to on a Saturday. Not my boss.

"I was totally just going to call you," I say as soon as I answer.

"What are you eating?"

"A delicious sausage."

"Interesting," she says in a singsong voice. "That's

exactly why I'm calling you." I can hear her collapsing onto a bed. "So, I'm tidying up Piper's room because she's out. And one of her notebooks just happened to fall on the floor."

"Uh-huh."

"And you know how I discovered a few months ago that she writes fanfiction?"

"You mean how you discovered it by making her notebooks *accidentally* fall open on the floor?"

"I'm very clumsy. It can't be helped. Anyway. Last time she was writing a very PG-13 *Stranger Things* fanfic story. Now she's working on something about Maddie and Declan."

Whaaaaat?

"Who is Declan, and why does your niece think you should be kissing him?"

"I have no idea, because I know for a fact that I should *not* be kissing him." I scoff, very convincingly. "She met Declan the other day. He's my asshole boss."

"*Really?* Because he doesn't sound like an asshole to me."

"Let me guess—does he sound like a man with a perfect butt?"

"Yes, but he also gazes at you longingly with his beautiful amber eyes."

"That is definitely fictional. You know for a fact that Piper has a hyperactive imagination."

"There has to be something there, or she wouldn't be shopping you."

"Shopping us?"

"Rooting for the two of you to succeed in a romantic relationship. *Maclan.*"

I have to laugh at that. "You mean *shipping.* She's shipping us. You know I love that girl, but she is absolutely flooded with hormones right now. She would root for two pigeons to succeed in a romantic relationship if she saw them sitting together."

"She's actually very perceptive."

"Yeah. She's extremely perceptive about boys' butts. You do realize we're talking about the man who's making me work on Christmas Day?"

"Oh yeah. That's still happening, huh?"

"Yeah. Still happening."

"But you'll be at Aunt Mel's for dinner?"

"Please—I tell *youse,*" I say, imitating our Aunt Mel from Staten Island. "I am there, come hell or high *watta, arright?*"

"*Youse betta* be, I'm tellin' *youse*… Shit. Piper's home. We never had this conversation—but we aren't done talking about Boss Butt!"

She ends the call.

That kid. I have no idea what Piper is thinking. *Maclan.*

I open up my messages app and scroll through the many, many text conversations with Declan. He definitely does not look at me longingly with his beautiful amber eyes. But he is kind of fun to text with. And look at. But terrible to work for. I can't even imagine how awful he'd be to date.

Suddenly, a new text notification pops up. From Boss Butt.

. . .

DECLAN: Happy Saturday, Cooper. You at home?

"Shit!"

DECLAN: I'm just asking if you're at home.

"Shit shit shit."

ME: Why do you ask?
DECLAN: Because I'm in the neighborhood.

I burst out laughing. Is he kidding me? What is this—a booty call? Am I supposed to get all excited? I tell him I'm at home, and he'd say, *Oh good, so you're not busy—I need you to do something for me.* "Not falling for it," I mumble to myself.

ME: I'm out running errands all day. And night. Unfortunately.
DECLAN: Really? Because your landlady let me in and I'm standing outside the door to

your apartment right now. Pretty sure I heard a woman swearing and laughing in there. Should I call the cops? Maybe someone broke in.

"Shit."

DECLAN: I think I just heard her again. Kind of a potty mouth. Sounds like trouble.
ME: Just tell me right now if you're here to murder me.
DECLAN: That depends on how long you're going to make me wait out here.

For purely professional reasons, I run to my bathroom, as quietly as possible.

ME: Could you first explain why I have the honor of receiving you at my home on a Saturday?

I roll a little perfume oil onto some pulse points and floss my teeth and gargle with mouthwash and apply lip gloss. Because my mother and my landlady would be appalled if they knew I received a gentleman caller without having done so. Even if the gentleman is my stinker of a boss.

DECLAN: I'm considering letting you have Christmas off.
ME: Go on...
DECLAN: And there's something I'd like to discuss with you. Something that I didn't want to discuss with you at the office. Something that is not work-related.

Gulp.

DECLAN: There's a legal agreement involved. It's not creepy.
ME: I'll be the judge of that.
DECLAN: Exactly how large of an apartment do you live in? Because it's taking you a really long time to reach the door.

I reach the door and open it. And *Scrooge me*, he might look even better unshaven, in a beanie, jeans, and black puffy jacket than he does all groomed in a suit and fancy wool trench coat. What an asshole.

"Hello, Magdalena."

"Only Mrs. Pavlovsky gets to call me that."

"Hello, Cooper… May I?" He gestures, asking if he can enter my home. Like a vampire. Like a vampire who smells like camping sex in a forest when it rains.

"Do I have a choice?"

"I'm about to present you with a choice, actually," he says as he brushes past me, pulling the beanie off and combing his fingers through his perfectly tousled chestnut brown hair. Like a vampire with bedhead.

He doesn't stop near the entrance to look around my apartment like most normal humans would—he immediately starts strolling around, checking it out. My living room area, the kitchen, the bathroom, and then peeks into my bedroom—as if he were at an open house. "This is pretty nice," he says, sounding surprised.

"You were expecting me to live in a hovel? Just because my work environment is wretched and unpleasant, that doesn't mean my home has to be."

And there's that damn dimple again.

Just as I realize I haven't shut my front door yet, my landlady pops her head in. "I very like *zis* man, Magdalena. Wonderful man to have for you," she enunciates while beaming at Declan.

"Very good, Mrs. Pavlovsky!" I praise her. "But I do not *have* this man, thank you."

"Thank you, Mrs. Pavlovsky," the man says, grinning. "I very like your building."

Why is he so nice to her? First my niece, now my landlady.

"Ohhh, *sank* you." She gives a little wave. Her cheeks are so flushed, she looks like Mrs. Claus. "Okay, I am leaving now. Bye-bye!"

I carefully shut the door and stay near it because I expect to be opening it and ushering Declan out shortly. "I'd offer to take your hat and coat, but I'm sure you won't be staying long."

He shoves his beanie into a pocket, unzips his coat very slowly while holding my gaze, and all I can do is stare at his bare hands and imagine him stripping naked. I blame my thirteen-year-old niece for this. But *God*, that man knows how to take off a coat. He shrugs it off and drapes it over one arm. "I'll keep it with me, in case I need to make a run for it."

"Good thinking."

"Can we sit down and talk for a minute?"

"Must we?"

"Are you this apprehensive with all of your guests?"

"No."

He smiles, shaking his head, hangs his puffy jacket on the back of a chair, and takes a seat at my dining table. "Have a seat, Maddie."

I get all tingly when he calls me Maddie. He almost never does. I can't tell if they're the good kind of tingles or not, but I can't seem to make them stop. I take a seat opposite him, and we're both watching each other's every move. He pulls a manila envelope from an inside coat pocket and places it on the table but doesn't pass it to me.

"How are you?" he asks as an afterthought, but he *almost* seems concerned.

"I'm apprehensive. How are you?"

"Eager to get down to it."

I take a deep, shaky breath and wait for him to proceed.

He gently places the fingers of his right hand on top of the envelope, staring down at it. "I realize you're unhappy with the idea of working so much during the holidays, and I'd like to propose a compromise… It turns out I have to attend a few family gatherings over the course of the next couple of weeks… A family dinner in Ohio on Christmas Eve. And a rehearsal dinner and family wedding on the 30th and 31st of December—which is a ridiculous date for a wedding, but there you go." He looks up at me as if this is all he needs to say.

"*And?*"

"And I would like you to attend these events with me."

"As your assistant?"

"As my date."

"*What?*"

"I would like you to pretend to be my girlfriend—with no obligation of fulfilling any of the actual duties of a girlfriend, other than to accompany me and behave like my girlfriend when we're around my family." He watches me for a response, but I am not giving him one. "In exchange for this, you do not have to work at the office from the 23rd until January 4th. But if you should choose to join me whenever I'm working there, it would be appreciated."

I just stare at this man, incredulous. I know that in a situation like this, the best thing to do would be to remain silent and make the other guy so uncomfortable that he starts to sweeten the deal. Or at least admit that he's hardly presenting me with a compromise at all. But I can't. I am not genetically programmed to remain silent.

"Is this a joke?"

"Is it funny?"

"I'm not laughing."

"And as an attorney, I would never joke about a potentially hazardous situation with an employee, even when it's regarding nonwork activities."

"Well, as an executive assistant, I foresee a number of problems with the proposed scenario, and I would like to prevent them by saying—*are you seriously for real right now?* You want your family to think that *I'm* your girlfriend?"

"Yes."

"You want me to lie to your family?"

"Yes."

"Why?"

"Because I promised my mother that I would attend these events, and she is under the impression that I have a girlfriend."

"Why would she have that impression?"

"Because I told her I have a girlfriend."

"And you *don't* have a girlfriend?"

"What do *you* think?"

"You want me to lie about being your assistant?"

"That's not necessary. We'll be in Ohio. It's highly unlikely that word would get back to anyone at the company that we're dating, so I think it's plausible that we'd gotten to know each other this way and that we'd handled it in the proper manner with HR and with my superior."

I narrow my eyes at him. "Why me?"

"Because, as you know, I don't have time to deal with a woman I've already been intimate with."

"'*Already*' been intimate with?"

"*Been* intimate with. You know what I mean."

"Yeah. Ohhhh, yeah. I know what you mean. You are unbelievable, sir."

He finally opens the envelope and slides one piece of paper toward me, and then pulls his Montblanc pen out from his inside jacket pocket. The one he uses to sign important documents. His lucky pen.

"Obviously we would have to refrain from discussing this matter in the workplace. Before, during, and after this limited period of time. With each other and certainly not with anyone else."

"Oh, trust me, I don't want to discuss this at all. *Ever*. I don't want to be discussing it with you right now."

"Really? Because you strike me as the kind of woman who can be straightforward and moderately rational when it comes to sex."

"Really? Because you strike me as the kind of man

who's totally oblivious about what women are thinking and feeling most of the time."

There's a flicker of something that looks like hurt in his eyes for a moment.

Suddenly he seems so vulnerable, and I feel unsure about absolutely everything.

Does Declan Cannavale have feelings?

But then he shakes his head and sets his jaw and offers me no more than a cocky grin as a response, and I'm right back to wanting to wipe the floor with his perfect boss butt.

SEVEN

Declan

THE FIRST NO WAY IN HELL

I know what you're thinking and feeling, Maddie Cooper. Even when you don't.

She's absolutely right. In my personal life, as it turns out, I *don't* always know what women are thinking or feeling. Or maybe just one woman. But I don't think about that woman anymore.

However, I can read Maddie like a dirty book. I know she's been suspicious of me for the past couple of days because I was being nice to her at work. I know it made her uncomfortable. I know how much easier it is for her to deal with me when she feels the need to put me in my place.

I'm starting to hear a little bit of that Staten Island accent again when she's mad, and I like it.

Merry Christmas to me.

She's got this place all decorated, and that twinkling Christmas tree is finally putting me in the holiday spirit. Or maybe it's because those big sparkly brown eyes of hers, they're glaring. Those nostrils, they're flaring. She's squirming around in her chair because her thighs are squeezing together. It's a beautiful sight. She's conflicted, and she's putting up a fight.

I am so glad she didn't agree to this ridiculous idea of mine right away.

I mean, I'll get her to come around eventually. But I wouldn't want her around if she were a pushover. She's not a pushover. And I really want her around.

And she'll feel better about agreeing to this shit show charade if she explicitly refuses first.

She finally glances down at the document, and it looks like she kind of wants to laugh, but she can't. "You want me to acknowledge that this *discreet, temporary, simulated consensual romantic relationship during nonworking hours* will not interfere with Sentinel's company policy of teamwork and a harmonious work environment."

God, I love it when she recites the terms I've written.

"I do."

"And you want me to acknowledge that the discreet, temporary, simulated consensual romantic relationship is not a misuse of your authority over me as an employee and thus cannot be perceived as favoritism or sexual harassment."

"Do you require further clarification of the terms?"

"I require a blunt object, followed by a stiff drink."

"I'd be happy to wait for you to consume one stiff drink before proceeding with this discussion."

"I think I'd be happier if you had come here to murder me."

"Aww, Coop. I'd never do that. I like having you around."

"You like *bossing* me around." She slides the piece of paper away.

"Not half as much as *you* like bossing *me* around." I wink. "And I don't mind it either. You've been an ideal executive assistant and partner at work. Which is why I think you'd be the most tolerable option as a date right now."

She blows out a laugh. "Wow. I mean, I can handle the wink, Mr. Cannavale. But I really start to tremble when you lay the sweet talk on that thick." She gets up from the table and starts pacing around.

I have conflicting emotions about this because now I can see her ass in those jeans, and I'm trying to make this agreement appear as safe and unsexy as possible. But I want to spank that ass. In a very sexy way.

It's problematic.

"This is not a compromise," she continues. "You just want me to work with you in an alternate manner, in alternate locations. I would be spending just as much time with you as I would if I had to work at the office through Christmas."

"It wouldn't be work. It might actually be fun for

you. I mean, it will be a nonstop living hell for me, but you'll probably find my family very entertaining."

"I'm not going to find your family anything. What makes you think I'd actually agree to any of this?"

I angle the chair so I can face her, spreading my legs apart and leaning forward. "Maddie. You sound angry," I say in a kind voice.

"Don't you attempt to present yourself with open and understanding body language. Don't label my emotions in an attempt to dissipate them. You think I don't know every negotiation tactic ever invented? You're trying to turn me into some kind of escort."

I am so glad she didn't fall for that.

"Not a *professional* escort—I have no intention of paying you for your company. I will, however, pay for all travel, food, and accommodations. Although, of course you will be the one to arrange all of it. I will pay for these things with money, and I will pay for them by tolerating your glares and sarcasm, as always." I give her a cute little blink and a dimpled smile.

She's not falling for it.

Good.

"Uh-huh." She stomps over, leans over the table, and points at the document. She's wearing her hair long and wild today, and my hands should be all up in there. "What is this clause you've initialed here? That you agree to not sue or terminate my services in the event that I should attempt or successfully manage to seduce you? Exactly how drunk were you when you typed this up?"

"I was sober enough to remember the very important bargaining tactic known in the legal community as 'tit for tat.' You'll see that I have also included here that you too will agree not to sue me or quit in the event that you should attempt or successfully manage to seduce me."

"Did you just use the word 'tit' while discussing my hypothetical attempts at seducing you? What is wrong with you?"

"Very little. When discussing nonwork relationships with women, I find it best to be up-front about things. It would be foolish to deny the fact that we're both attractive, single individuals. In legal terms, we are what's known as *hot as fuck.* This will be an isolated period of time in which we'll be interacting with each other in more casual environments than we're accustomed to. You might accidentally drink spiked eggnog and get a little frisky."

"I hate eggnog," she hisses.

"You also claim to hate me, and I'm not refuting that. But it's the holidays. The holidays stir up feelings in everyone. It's inevitable. To be clear—I am not saying this has to happen. I'm acknowledging the potential for these circumstances. There will be alcohol. You'll be seeing me in a new context, and chances are good that you'll want to have sex with me. And I, for one, do not wish for such circumstances to result in the end of our working relationship if they should occur once or several times."

"Are you saying there's no chance that *you'll* want

to have sex with *me* due to these hypothetical circumstances?"

"I am definitely not saying that. I wouldn't say that. But until you sign this, I won't say that I want to."

She shakes her head, and there's so much anger and adrenaline coursing through her veins that I'm pretty sure she could flip me and this table over right now. But I just want to bend her over it. "Fucking lawyers."

"Fucking right. I like having you as my assistant, Cooper. But I need you to accompany me to these family events. And I want to minimize the potential impact on our ability to work together. That is why I require a signed agreement stating that we will not let this interfere with our fantastic work relationship. Come what may."

"*'Come what may?'* Exactly how drunk are you right now?"

"I had a beer at McSorley's on my way over."

She barks out a laugh. "Sure you did."

McSorley's Old Ale House is an awesome old timey Irish pub just down the street from this building. It's kind of a dive, a little touristy, and the exact opposite kind of a place that I usually go to when I'm in New York. But that doesn't mean I wouldn't go there.

"I'm half Irish. Why wouldn't I?"

"Because your shoes cost more than the décor and furniture in that place."

"Faulty logic, Coop. I can go anywhere in these

shoes. And I suddenly felt the need for a dark ale before facing you."

"Don't call me Coop. It warms my heart that the prospect of seeing me would drive you to drink, but they only serve two mugs of beer at a time at McSorley's."

"I know. I gave one to the guy who was next to me at the counter. I clinked glasses with him, and I said..." I give her my best Irish accent and prepare to catch her when she swoons because it always brings the ladies to their knees. "'May the winds of fortune sail you. May you sail a gentle sea. May it always be the other guy who says this drink's on me.' And then he said, 'Here's to a long life and a merry one. A quick death and an easy one. A pretty girl and an honest one. A cold beer and another one.'" And then I wink at her for good measure.

She narrows her eyes at me, and her fists go straight to her hips. "Don't you try to brogue me into complying either, Cannavale. I wasn't born yesterday."

Fair play. Tough customer. "Maddie, I'm not drunk right now. And I'm not lying. And I need an answer."

"Well then, my answer is no. No way. No way in hell."

That's my girl.

"Okay." My work here is done. I stand up and put my jacket back on. "You still have time to think about it." I slide the beanie back on, watching her watch my hands the whole time. *Yeah. Get a good look at these hands and think long and hard about what you want me to do with them over the holidays.*

"I will not be thinking about it."

"Yeah you will."

Do I actually think our working relationship would survive a few rounds of hot vacation sex? Yeah. I do. She may not know who she's dealing with here, but I do. And she can handle it.

"Why would I agree to this?"

"Would you rather be at the office with me on Christmas Day than spend a couple of days and evenings with me in nonwork environments and get some much-needed time off?"

"If you're going to these events, then it is clearly not as dire for you to work through Christmas as you had led me to believe."

"I'll have to make up for lost time, and I'll be working at the office even when you aren't there."

"*Really?* You'll be working at the office without me? All by yourself?"

I shrug. "If I have to, yeah," I say quietly, my shoulders slouching the tiniest bit. Because I am not above trying to make her feel sorry for me right now.

"You know what?" she says. "Thank you for the offer, Mr. Cannavale. I'll think about it."

I study her poker face. "You will?"

She smirks and leans toward me. "You sound skeptical."

I fucking love that smirk.

I know what she's doing. She thinks she'll have some kind of power over me if she doesn't give me an answer one way or another. Look how happy she is right now.

"Okay, Cooper." I put my gloves on. "You think about it."

"I shall." She nods once. "When do you need to know by?"

She needs a deadline. Deadlines for accepting offers are always tricky, but I have a feeling this woman needs as much time as possible to warm up to this idea. "The 22nd. Six pm. But I'll need you to book travel and accommodations for us ASAP. You can always cancel your flights if necessary." And before she can open that gorgeous, sassy mouth, I continue. "Separate adjoining rooms at the Ritz-Carlton in Cleveland."

She frowns as she opens the door to the hallway. "You're not going to stay with your family?"

"Absolutely not."

"But they don't live right in Cleveland, do they?"

"No, they don't. But the best hotels are there, and I always stay at the Ritz-Carlton. And we're only staying one night. The night of the 24th. Fly in that afternoon. Fly out the next morning. That's very important. The wedding's in Cleveland, so we'll stay there for that too. I'll email you the info."

She's still frowning at me, and as I pass her on my way out the door, I have the strongest urge to grab her and kiss that mouth. *Really* give her something to frown about. But I won't. There's no kissing in the art of negotiating a deal. And I need this. I need her. I need her for *this*.

"Uh-huh. And if I decline your offer, will you be traveling alone or selecting some other lucky hot-as-fuck winner?"

God, I love it when she says hot as fuck.

"I'll probably just cancel everything. I mean, I have to go to the wedding, but…"

"Whose wedding is it, anyway?"

Now I'm frowning. Now I hate everything again. "My brother's. See you Monday."

I can hear her sigh of exasperation, followed by a derisive scoff, as I stride down the hall away from her. She thinks I'm being a moody asshole as usual, and that's fine. I'll be having flowers sent to Mrs. Pavlovsky—to thank her for letting me in today. And to keep Cooper's nosey landlady on my team.

Art of the deal.

Deal with it, Maddie Cooper.

EIGHT

Piper

MADDIE AND DECLAN, SITTIN' IN A CHRISTMAS TREE

K-i-s-s-i-n-g. That's what they were doing. With their eyes and their words.

They would kiss with their lips eventually.

It was fate.

Maclan was just a couple waiting to happen.

A love story waiting to be written.

Why did it have to wait, one might wonder?

Why could Maddie not see the way Declan gazed at her longingly with his beautiful amber eyes? Why could she not see the chemistry between them? It was hot enough to melt the North Pole.

So was Declan's butt.

His perfect, perfect butt.

It was the most perfect man butt Maddie had ever seen, even though she refused to admit it to herself or anyone else.

He had the Holy Grail of butts.

But back to Maddie.

What was holding her back?

It wasn't a lack of confidence.

Oh no—that lady had confidence to spare.

It wasn't that she was blind—even she could see how gorgeous Declan was.

Maybe it was just that she was so busy looking over her shoulder at all the crappy boyfriends from her past that she couldn't see the potentially great boyfriend that was standing right in front of her desk all along. Or for two months or whatever. A New York minute was like a second, but two months was basically forever in the world of New York dating. It's weird.

That was why Christmas was the perfect time for Declan to take Maddie matters into his own hands—to take Maddie into his own hands…under the mistletoe.

It was their company's holiday party—a day unlike any other day. It was a day of celebration—of the baby Jesus but also of love. And that's what it was for Maddie and Declan. It was love. Maddie just didn't know it yet. As she was gathering up her things to go home, she also did not know it yet, but she was about to get the greatest Christmas present anyone would ever give her (except for the macaroni portrait of her face that her awesome niece had given her several years ago).

She said good night and happy holidays to the super nice receptionist, but she didn't bother saying goodbye to Declan, because she knew he would just text her as soon as she was gone. He always texted her. That's what boys do when they like a girl. Everyone knows that. But for some reason, Maddie didn't understand that when her boss texted her to ask her to do things for him—what he was actually doing was asking her to be his girlfriend. Showing her that she was always on his mind.

She was leaving the party early because she was going to go shopping for some amazing presents for her favorite niece—she was going to get her at least three of the items listed on the Google document that her niece had shared with her and the rest of their family. So, it was just her standing there in the lobby, by the elevators. She had been so busy thinking about the presents she would be buying her niece that she didn't even notice the mistletoe that was hanging right above her.

"Where do you think you're going?" Declan said from right behind her.

She rolled her eyes and turned to face him. She was about to say something sassy to him, as usual, but she didn't get the chance because Declan's mouth was on her mouth. He kissed her and kissed her, until they both had to catch their breaths. That was when he said, "Merry Christmas, Maddie. I love you."

"You do?" she asked. Her eyes were filling with tears, but she could finally see him clearly. She could finally see herself clearly. "Well, now that you mention it, I love you too."

And then they kissed again. Passionately.

Their lips were locking while everyone else was rocking around the Christmas tree.

It was a good thing no one else at the party was paying attention to them, because they were really going at it. Declan's hands were all up in her luxurious brown hair, and Maddie's hands were clinging to his incredible butt. There just happened to be paparazzi hiding behind a big plant, so pictures of their PDA ended up all over the internet, and that was fine with them. Because neither of them wanted to hide their love from the world or, more importantly, from each other anymore.

The elevator dinged and the doors opened. Just as their hearts were opening, to each other. They got inside the empty elevator together without even pausing their kiss. When the elevator doors closed, Declan hit the stop button so the doors would stay closed. An alarm went off, but they couldn't even hear it over the sound of their beating hearts. They kissed even harder and more, like with tongues and hands and legs and stuff.

They were suspended midair, and New York time was finally standing still.

And that's how it happened. First came love. Then came marriage. Maddie's niece was the most beautiful bridesmaid the world had ever known (and that was how she met her future husband Shawn Mendes, who performed at their wedding). And then, eventually, would come a baby in a baby carriage. But not for a long time, because there were already enough babies in the family for now. But when they do have a baby, they will give it the middle name Piper and make Piper the godmother because they realize just how important she is in their lives, now and forevermore.

NINE

Declan

COCKY AROUND THE CHRISTMAS TREE

Socks.

Nobody ever *asks* for socks. Not for Christmas, anyway. I never had to because my nonna gives me socks every year. She gives everyone socks, every year. But she presents us with really nice socks. Italian socks. Because she's so busy cooking during the holidays that she doesn't have time to shop for unique gifts for each individual. So everyone always gets socks. It's a family tradition. It's charming.

But Drucker was just being a lazy dick when he wrapped this three-pack of gold toe crew socks and stuck a label with my name on it. We aren't doing that thing where we have to guess who our Secret Santa was, thank Christ. But I know it was him. Because he's a lazy dick who just happened to have closed a twenty-eight-million-dollar deal this week—a deal that I saved. Because it's my job to save this company's ass from assholes and idiots and lazy dicks. And what do I get? A pat on the back from my CEO, a massive year-end bonus, socks, and nothing.

I haven't gotten what I actually want for Christmas, anyway.

Or need.

But I'll get it. I just didn't expect to feel this nervous about it, now that it's getting down to the wire. Five-fifteen on the 22nd of December and absolutely no indication that Maddie will be accompanying me to Ohio. She's booked everything, although she didn't do exactly as I'd asked her to. Because she knows that as of now, I've got no leverage. It's problematic. And still weirdly hot that she's pushing the envelope like this.

Instead of flying in on the afternoon of the 24th, she booked us on separate flights to Cleveland—tomorrow. When I complained, she told me that she was just being a good assistant, as usual. It's the winter, and there's always a chance that the weather will prevent me from arriving at my destination on time. Better safe than sorry, she said. And we wouldn't want to risk being seen together at the airport in NYC, so to be safe—separate flights. And she might not even be on hers. She booked her flight "just in case."

She did not book us adjoining suites at the Ritz-Carlton in Cleveland either. She didn't book us into the Ritz-Carlton or any of the hotels in Cleveland for the 23rd and 24th. She booked rooms at a hotel in Youngstown. An hour and fifteen minutes from Cleveland. Ten minutes from my parents' house. "I know it feels like I did this to punish you," she said, "but it's just to be safe."

And I'm not mad. I'm a lawyer—I respect being safe. I respect her audacity. It looks good on her. Everything looks good on her. Especially that bright red dress. It clings to her audacious curves like the skin of a Red Delicious apple, and I am staying just as close to her at this party. To be safe. I wouldn't want her to feel like she has to wave off lazy dick fruit flies like Drucker on her own. I'm here to help.

Shapiro, our CEO, is wearing a four-thousand-dollar suit and a crappy Santa hat, passing out Secret Santa gifts to his employees. I'm pretending to give a shit while three assistants sing some fucking Jonas Brothers Christmas song on the karaoke machine. On top of the deluxe karaoke machine, Shapiro sprung for the back room of this fancy steakhouse that's a few blocks from our offices. He's not buying us steak, but there's an open bar. I advised him to give out drink tickets and enforce a two-drink maximum per guest, but he didn't listen. It's fine. The off-site venue reduces the company's liability, and the professional bartenders know when to cut people off. But he did take my advice and provided safe transportation options for anyone who needs it. This is why you should never invite your general counsel to your office holiday party. And why I shouldn't be here. Because I'm always on the lookout for potential legal issues.

I gotta hand it to whoever decorated this place, though. With the strings of lights and the sparkly snowflakes and the very appropriate hanging blue balls and the silver tree—it looks nice. If you like this sort of shiny, happy holiday thing. *I don't.* But I respect it.

What I don't respect is lazy dick assholes who think they can hit on my assistant just because she's wearing a bright red dress and hasn't told them to fuck off yet. Just because she's standing right behind me there, politely listening to him word-vomit about how relaxing it is at his beach house in the Hamptons in the winter. She knows I'm listening—that's why she keeps *oohing* and *ahhing*, as if she's actually considering accepting this d-bag's invitation to hang out with him there. As if that's a more enticing option than dinner with my family in Ohio.

"Well, let me know," Drucker says. "I'm heading up there tomorrow, for a week. In case you don't already have plans. Should be super chill."

"I'll think about it, thanks," she replies. "I haven't quite decided what I'm going to do yet. But it certainly sounds more relaxing than *some* of my options."

She *accidentally on purpose* elbows me in the back, almost making me spill the drink in my hand. Almost. I put the tumbler down on the buffet table next to us and turn to join in on the conversation, because she obviously wants me to—just as Drucker is pulling something out of his blazer pocket.

"Hey, what's *this* doing in here?" he exclaims, like the world's worst close-up magician. He holds up a sprig of fake mistletoe, and before he can say *why don't you help me honor this holiday tradition,* I've swiped that thing out of his hand and crumpled it up. "What the shit, man?" he whines.

"As general counsel of this firm, I'd advise against the use of mistletoe at a work function."

Maddie covers her mouth to keep from laughing out loud.

"It's not like I was going to force her to do anything," he mumbles.

"Best not to put her in an awkward position to begin with."

Now she's laughing out loud.

Yeah, I get the irony.

But at least I waited until non-office hours to approach her and offered her the safety of a legal agreement instead of a leafy invitation to sexual harassment. And also—this guy is neither hot as fuck, nor is he physically or mentally agile enough to appreciate or handle her in all the ways she deserves to be handled.

"Employers are legally liable, even when incidents occur at off-site venues. Thanks for the socks, by the way." I wave them around in front of Drucker's face.

"What makes you think they're from me?" he asks, grinning like a lazy dick sock-giver.

"Got you written all over it. What'd *you* get, Cooper?"

"A twenty-dollar gift card for White Castle!"

"From onion rings guy?"

"It even smells like onion rings." She giggles, holding the card up under my nose.

"Mmm, reminds me of the interior of my car," I say in a hushed voice—because this is an inside joke between my assistant and me and has nothing to do with Drucker.

"I love White Castle," he says. "I like their smoothies."

And before he can suggest that they stop by there on the way to the Hamptons, Maddie gets called over to the karaoke machine, because apparently, she signed up for a song.

"Hold this for me, will you?" She smirks, placing the card in the palm of my hand.

She smooths down the front of her dress as she sashays over to grab a mic and then proceeds to sing "You're A Mean One, Mr. Grinch." To me. Like Marilyn Monroe singing "Happy Birthday, Mr. President." Except instead of wishing me a happy birthday, she's telling me, in front of everyone, that my heart is an empty hole and she wouldn't touch me with a thirty-nine-and-a-half-foot pole.

Which is hilarious.

I mean—*I'm* laughing. Everyone's laughing. I don't even care that Drucker's laughing.

Because it's a holiday party. And her sexy voice is filling this entire room with holiday spirit and good old-fashioned sass. It's not even sass, really. She's cocky as hell. She isn't nervously checking her watch to see how much time she has left to decide if she wants to accompany her boss to a few enjoyable family functions or work at the office all day and night for the rest of the year. And neither am I.

I'm cool as a Christmas pickle. A pickle who might have to call his mom and tell her his new girlfriend just got hit by a truck. Or maybe *I'll* get hit by a truck. I could get lucky. I still believe in Christmas miracles. My heart isn't really an empty hole. It's an *ass*hole. And an idiot. But it's not a lazy dick.

I applaud and hoot and holler when Maddie's done serenading me. She gives me a big, toothy grin from across the room. Service with a smile, always. But that smile falters for a moment. As she's handing the microphone to someone else, those big brown eyes are still fixed on mine. I don't know what my face is doing right now, but it's making her a little worried. About me. About how she's made me feel, maybe.

She cares. She doesn't like it. But she cares.

What do you know? I might just have to look both ways when I cross the road on the way back to Sentinel so I *don't* get hit by a truck. I might just have something to live for.

I tear my eyes away from her and stroll on over to the open bar to get one more drink before I head back to the office. I nod at What's-Her-Name from Down the Hall, and Broker from the Downtown Office with the Stupid Mustache. It's great to see everyone here at this party. Just great.

"Another Jameson," I order from the bartender. "Neat."

Shapiro calls out to Cindy, the unbearably happy receptionist, and tells her she's going to have to come over to him to open up her present. Because it's so huge. He had a bunch of interns bring all eighty of the Secret Santa gifts over from the office, but he isn't willing to carry one twenty-one-pound box over to a sweet middle-aged lady in a Rudolph sweater. I am not the only one who's watching her open this big box —it's bigger than all the others. Nobody's jealous, though, because Cindy deserves it. She's the heart of the corporate office. It's annoying how relentlessly cheerful she is, but she means well.

She screams—actually screams—as soon as she tears off the wrapping and sees the top of the box. It's one of those deluxe karaoke machines from Korea. She loves karaoke. Everyone knows this. Sure, it cost a little more than the twenty-dollar limit. Okay, it cost over eight hundred dollars more than the limit. What are they gonna do? Sue for overspending and being a more awesome gift-giver than everyone else? As general counsel, I'd advise against it.

Cindy is so happy, and for some reason, Maddie appears to be really happy for her. She goes over to hug her. Cindy's crying. Happy tears—you'd think Justin Timberlake jumped out of the box and kissed her—but she's crying. Which is awkward. She wants to know who her Secret Santa is, but no one's coming forward to claim the reward for being the greatest guy at Sentinel and possibly in all of Manhattan.

Because seeing Cindy happy is reward enough.

I gulp down my whiskey, check my personal phone. There's a text from my buddy Matt, asking if I'll be at his party. I tell him I won't be able to make it out to Brooklyn tonight. There's a text from my sister, with a photo attachment of something deep-fried that our nonna is making her family for dinner. It might be a thumb. There's a text from someone who has no business texting me now or ever again. I delete it without reading it. And I have no idea how long Cooper has been standing right behind me, but she keeps saying my name.

"Hi," I say, shoving the phone back into my pocket. She looks like she's about to tell me something really important.

And I am ready to hear it.

"There you are," Drucker says, handing her a cup. "Try this. It's incredible."

She takes the cup from him, still staring at me, at whatever my face is doing. She takes a big gulp and then—spits it out. All over my shirt.

Merry fucking Christmas to me.

TEN

Maddie

SATAN BABY

What a baby.

Scratch the surface of every gorgeous, cocky man in this city, and that's what you get. A big baby. Okay, so I sang a song about how mean he is in front of everyone we work with. It was a joke. It's not like he cares what people think of him. Okay, so I spewed eggnog all over his beautiful face and shirt. It was an accident.

I immediately offered to take the shirt to the cleaners for him. But he just pulled those socks that Drucker had given him out of his jacket pocket, dabbed at his face and shirt with them, and left. Didn't say goodbye. He didn't even find it a little bit funny. It's not like I had done it on purpose to make him laugh—but *come on.*

And to think I was feeling badly for him after I saw the look on his face when I had finished singing the Grinch song. Those sad eyes. That expression of—what? Longing? Wistfulness? It was so unlike him. I thought I was getting a glimpse into his soul for once.

To think I was about to tell him I would go with him to Ohio. Pretend to be his girlfriend for a few days. Because I do realize what a bind he must be in if he actually asked me to do this. He doesn't take things like this lightly. That's why he's a good lawyer. But that doesn't make him a good person. It's not like he sent flowers to my landlady because he's such a sweet guy. I know how he thinks. He did it because he knew she'd be all up in my face about him. And she has been. Ever since last weekend.

First my niece and now my landlady. It's one thing to have to deal with him at work, but I can't even pretend to like someone who's that uptight. Not that *I'm* the life of every party. Not that I even want to go to every party. But if I'm going to choose to go anywhere with anyone, it's got to be worth my precious time. I can't believe I actually came back to the office in the freezing cold just to check on him—I'm such a sucker. The fucker walks so fast, I couldn't catch up with him, and he didn't even reply to my texts.

It doesn't even make sense that he would be this mad because of the eggnog. Or the song. Or the fact that I haven't given him an answer yet. But I'm going to give him an answer. It's five to six, and he'll get his answer. He won't like it, and I'm actually a little concerned that he might fire me right now, but he'll get his answer.

Sentinel is eerily quiet when I step off the elevators. The temp receptionist nods at me, and I can just tell from her flushed cheeks and the intoxicating scent combination of tobacco and a sweet and spicy hot drink and sex on an antique leather sofa that Declan Cannavale has passed through here very recently. I can also tell that these temps were goofing off until we showed up.

Declan has the blinds inside his office *and* the door closed. I nod at the guy who's sitting at my desk and knock on the door before opening it. And *fuck me running on Santa's sled*—my boss doesn't have a shirt on, and he has the most stunning male torso I have ever seen.

I immediately shut the door behind myself, but I don't know what to say. I also can't seem to look away. Or breathe. Or calm my stupid lady parts down. We've never been glared at by a gorgeous, shirtless, infuriating man before. And I can't tell yet if it's the best or the worst thing that's happened to us yet, but it's a lot of things. I'm so glad I'm still wearing my coat so he can't tell that my nipples are trying to claw their way through my push-up bra and dress.

He continues to stare at me, unflinchingly, as he reaches into a desk drawer and pulls out one of his brand-new spare dress shirts. It's crisp and white, and he gives it a good snap to shake out the folds, startling me. I let out a gasp and lean back against the door, clutching the doorknob with one hand, squeezing my trembling thighs together. It's not like my breasts are heaving and I'm biting my lower lip or anything. I am perfectly capable of controlling my behavior. I can wait until I get home to do that stuff.

"Can I help you, Cooper?" he asks, finally looking away from me so he can carefully spread the shirt out on top of his desk and unbutton it.

He must exfoliate and moisturize the shit out of his skin, it's so smooth.

"I was just going to offer to take your shirt to the dry cleaners again."

"No thanks. Anything else?"

"Are you going back to the party?"

"I think I've had enough holiday fun for one day. Anything else?" He's back to glaring at me as he lifts up the shirt. When he raises one arm to slide it into a sleeve, I get a glimpse of a tattoo on the inside of his bicep. A bird. And *fuck me, it's beginning to look a lot like my Instagram feed in here.*

I clear my throat. "I've been thinking about your offer." I clear my throat again.

"And?"

"And I absolutely do not want to go with you to Ohio."

His eyelids flutter, and for one melancholy moment I think I'm getting a glimpse into his soul again. But then he tilts his head the tiniest bit and grins at me. "*But?*"

Cocky little…

"But I will."

He nods once, as if he knew I would all along. "Have you signed the document?"

I unzip my coat. Until this very minute, I wasn't

sure if I'd be shredding and burning the document or handing it over to him. But I've been carrying it with me all week. And I signed it as soon as I saw the crumpled-up receipt for the karaoke machine on his desk this afternoon. And the leftover wrapping paper in the corner. I knew it was a Secret Santa gift for Cindy. And when he didn't even claim responsibility for it at the party…

I stroll over, watch him watching me as he continues to button up his shirt. I stop directly in front of his desk, push my coat aside, and reach down into my cleavage to pull out the folded-up piece of paper. I hold it up between two fingers.

Not gonna lie to you. It feels good to watch that jaw clench. To see that vein along the side of his neck. To see his eyelids grow heavy and that Adam's apple bob up and down just once.

I drop that folded-up signed document onto his desk and turn on my heels and say, "I'm going home now. To pack. If you need anything, work-wise—let the temp know." Before opening the door, I stage whisper without looking back at him: "See you in Ohio, sweetheart."

I grab my laptop and bag from the locked drawer in my desk and answer a couple of questions for the temp, but then I make a quick exit. I don't even wait for the elevator. I would rather walk down seven flights of stairs in these heels than get caught after touching my boobs in front of my boss and dropping the mic like that.

Not that I don't think I can handle facing him

again. I graduated top of my class in Business Administration. I had six job offers before I'd even finished my exams. I've got recruiters trying to scout me all the time, even when I'm not looking… If shit gets real between us over the holidays, I'll have no trouble finding another job.

But I'm not worried.

I'll continue to have no trouble resisting him. As long as there's no alcohol. Or mistletoe. And he doesn't do anything terrible, like be nice to me or take off his shirt when I'm around or smile at me.

Merry fucking Christmas to me.

Chapter Eleven

DECLAN: Cooper. Did you specifically request that I be seated next to the most boring man on the plane?
MADDIE: Actually, he requested to be seated next to the grumpiest, most intolerable man on the plane. Sometimes things just work out. <woman shrugging emoji>
DECLAN: He just described every single thing he had to eat today. In great detail. He didn't have to. I could see it all between his teeth and on his jacket.
MADDIE: BE NICE!!!
DECLAN: I'm always nice, Cooper. Why don't you try being nicer to me for a change? It's sort of a requirement as my girlfriend. You should probably start practicing now.
MADDIE: This is me being nicer to you. I'm smiling at my phone right now. See?
MADDIE: <image sent>

DECLAN: Jesus. That's what you look like right now?
DECLAN: I mean, the finger was unnecessary. But fuck.
MADDIE: Would you care to register a complaint?
DECLAN: Yes. No one else should be able to see you looking that good. You should be sitting next to me right now.
MADDIE: Better safe than sorry. And I, for one, am not sorry.
DECLAN: You have a stopover at Dulles. You should be on this nonstop flight with me. It's stupid.
MADDIE: I'll be in Cleveland an hour and a half after you land. It's not that bed.
MADDIE: It's not that bad. <woman facepalming emoji>
DECLAN: Already thinking about getting into bed with me, huh? I like it.
DECLAN: But this arrangement is unnecessary and a waste of time, and it's already terrible. Who are you sitting next to? It better not be a guy.
MADDIE: Oops! Time to put the phones away. See you in C-town, hon! <winking face emoji>
DECLAN: That had better be sexty double entendre.
DECLAN: I will remind you that I've got dibs on your C-town until January 2nd, Cooper.

Potential, consensual DIBS.
DECLAN: Cooper.
DECLAN: Maddie.
DECLAN: Unacceptable. Text me when you get to Dulles and when you leave Dulles and when you land in Cleveland. And when you realize what a bad idea it was for us to travel separately. And when you realize how much you miss me.

TWELVE

Maddie

DASHING, THOUGH NO SNOW

I was expecting it to be cold in Cleveland. I'm not naïve—I knew that simply being in another city with Declan in a nonwork capacity would feel different. I have been mentally and emotionally preparing myself to handle any possible mood that he might be in and varying degrees of handsomeness depending on his wardrobe and facial hairiness.

But gosh darnit, nothing has prepared me for the sudden rise in body temperature and flood of hormones and emotions and bodily fluids triggered by seeing Declan Cannavale standing there in the arrivals concourse. He's holding up a hand-written airport pickup sign that says ***WELCOME TO C-TOWN, COOPER. GET YOUR ASS IN THE CAR—NOW!***

His lopsided grin is infuriating, his day-old scruff is mouthwatering, his suit and coat are elegant, and the slow journey his eyes are making from my bunhead down to the toes of my shiny high-heeled boots is agonizing. My ass is saying "Yes sir!" and I don't trust my mouth to say anything appropriate, so I keep it shut and just let him finish his extravagant visual sweep of my impossibly tight sweater dress.

I feel naked right now and he knows it, and it makes me want to slap him. And it makes me want to strip him naked and oil us both up so I can slide all over him or something. But I also don't want to give him the satisfaction of being right about me being attracted to him.

It's complicated.

"Took you long enough to disembark" is what he grumbles when he's finally done eye-banging me.

"I had to help a little old lady find her connecting flight," I tell him.

"Well, you didn't *have* to." There's a glint in his tea brown eyes—an evil sexy Christmas elf glint—as he reaches for my overnight bag. I allow him to take it from me, and the touch of his fingers on my shoulder sends tingles all the way down to my south pole. "Come on. Driver's waiting for us. Thanks for ordering a stretch limo, by the way. Baller move."

"Well, I just want to travel in the manner to which I have grown accustomed."

"Uh-huh."

Okay, so I haven't been in a stretch limo since prom, and I wanted to make my boss pay for one. I regret nothing. In particular, I do not regret ordering the white stretch limo with neon pink interior strip lighting and complimentary bottle of mediocre champagne because I knew how much he'd hate it. *And he does!* But it's not stopping him from knocking back the bubbly.

I'm sitting as far away from him as possible, in a seat that faces the bar and the small monitor. The TV screen currently features *A Christmas Story*. It's one of my favorite holiday movies, and it offers a very timely reminder of why I should never lick a frozen pole. Especially when it's attached to my boss.

He hasn't said a word to me since we climbed inside this monstrosity fifteen long minutes ago. He's just been typing on his laptop and occasionally glancing up at me to make sure that I'm as uncomfortable as he clearly wants me to be. But I'm not uncomfortable. I'm having a ring-a-ling-a-ding-dong-ding blast of a limo ride, and I'm not going to let him ruin it for me just because he's being a boring naughty-list-sack-of-coal.

"Aren't you even a little bit happy to be home?" I ask while staring at the TV monitor.

"I am a little bit happy to be home. Can't you tell?"

I turn to look at him and find him exactly as stone-faced as he was before.

"I wonder if your family is excited to see you. Do they all hate you too?"

"The word 'too' would imply that someone else hates me, Cooper. No one hates me. I mean, that old lady who was crossing the street that time hated me, but that was a misunderstanding. And that guy who threw his coffee at my car hated me, but he was just being a dick."

"Who? What are you talking about?"

"Irrelevant. In general, and in all ways that matter, I'm a nonstop fucking delight."

I purse my lips and turn my attention back to Ralphie and his family.

"You don't hate me, Coop. You hate how much you like me. Big difference."

"Not really."

"You'll see."

I shake my head, looking out the window in front of me, because *I can't even* with him right now. "So tell me about them."

"Who?"

"Your family. The people I will be meeting and lying to tomorrow."

"Right. We need to get our backstory straight." I can hear him grinning. "The most believable lies are always the ones that are mostly true. Which is why I think we should just say it was love at first sight. As soon as you met me."

Eye roll.

"I was professional. I resisted you for a solid week. But you pursued me in subtle yet irresistible ways, and I succumbed. I discussed and cleared the relationship with Shapiro and HR. We behave ourselves at the office, and very few of our co-workers know about your obsession with me. Simple. Believable. Almost true."

"Except the part about all of it."

"Except the parts that haven't happened yet."

Exaggerated eye roll.

I turn to him and say, "I don't feel very comfortable telling a lie of such magnitude."

"Okay, then. If you want to get even closer to the truth..." He looks away, shifting around in his seat, before continuing. "We can just say that I had a crush on you from even before the first time I saw you. It started when you were still working for Artie. When I'd call to talk to him. For a little while, the best part of my day was chatting with you on the phone for about thirty seconds. And now, the only bad parts of my day are when you aren't around. Or not responding to my texts."

Stunned silence.

I wait for him to burst out laughing, give me a sly, toothy grin—something. But he doesn't. Silence fills the gaudy, cavernous space around us, and it sounds something like the truth, only it's not any truth that I recognize as ours.

"Would that be easier for you to sell, Maddie?" He's staring down at his hands, and I wish I could read minds. I wish I could see into the future and know what would happen if I answered him with my lips and hands, because right now my whole body wants to tell him something that he deserves to know. Even if my own brain isn't willing to acknowledge it.

"Umm..."

"Would it?" He finally looks up at me.

I shake my head because the lump in my throat isn't going anywhere.

"Didn't think so," he says, shrugging it off like it's no big deal. "We'll figure something out when the time comes, I guess." He holds his empty glass out toward me.

I reach over to pour the champagne, taking in a shaky breath and clearing my throat. "You still haven't actually told me about your family."

"Right. We'll be having dinner at my parents' house. Mary Margaret and Tony Cannavale. They still live in the house I grew up in. My mom's from Boston. My dad grew up here. His mother—my nonna—is from Italy. She'll be there tomorrow. She's always here for the holidays. She'll hate you, but she hates everyone, so don't take it personally."

"Does she hate *you*?"

"Nobody hates me, Cooper, I told you. But she isn't nice to me. She isn't nice to anyone. All my brothers and my sister will be there, and their families. Aiden, Brady, Casey, and Eddie. Casey's the girl. Her daughter Penelope is my favorite person on the planet —try to contain your jealousy. Eddie's my baby brother."

"Aww." I'm picturing some adolescent boy around the same age as Piper. "How old is he?"

"Twenty-six," he deadpans. "He's an ugly little fucker and not at all charming—you won't like him. Women never like him," he says, trying not to smile "So he won't take it personally."

"Poor guy. Who are you closest to?"

He blinks and then polishes off his champagne in one big gulp. "What do you mean?"

"Which sibling are you closest to?"

He frowns, resting the glass on his knee. "It changes."

"Okay. What about now?"

"My sister, I guess. And Eddie. They're great. But stay away from Eddie. He's trouble."

"Please. I'm your girlfriend—what am I gonna do? Hit on your brother at Christmas dinner?"

And that's when any normal human would at least offer a polite fake laugh or a raised eyebrow perhaps, but Declan Cannavale's mood shifts, and I swear, the neon pink lighting flickers and it gets a little bit darker all around him. Men are always complaining that women are impossible to read—like the Sphynx. But sometimes this guy's thoughts are hieroglyphs written in invisible ink on papyrus and then folded up and shoved inside a flaming bag of dog poop. I could try stepping on the flaming bag of dog poop to put out the fire, but I'm still not going to be able to read that folded-up note inside.

"Is there anything else I should know about your family, Declan?"

He shakes his head. "If you have a specific question, just ask." He places the champagne glass on the strip of counter beside him and opens up his laptop again. "Otherwise, I'll be using the next hour of this drive to catch up on work."

"You're not going to ask me about the important people in *my* life?"

"Well, I already know about the *most* important person in your life." He points his thumbs at himself.

"And I already know about your parents. Carly and Joe Cooper. Right?"

"Yes. How did you know that?"

"I heard you say their names on the phone once when you were ordering something to be delivered to them on their anniversary. They live in Murray Hill."

"Yes."

"Which is where you grew up."

"Yes."

"But your mom's from Staten Island, and you have at least one aunt who still lives there."

"Yes."

"Your sister Rebecca is your best friend, and her daughter Piper is adorable and has a massive crush on me."

"Bex. I call my sister Bex. How do you know all that? Did you do a background check on me or something?"

"Sure, if paying attention and remembering things counts as a background check. I don't know if you know this, but you're kind of a loudmouth, Coop. I can always hear you yammering when I'm in my office with the door open."

"My apologies. I guess I didn't think you were listening."

"My apologies," he mumbles, staring at his laptop screen. "I guess I thought you wanted me to hear."

And I don't even know what to say about that, so I turn my attention back to Ralphie and his family. I honestly do not understand this man. And I don't understand why I want to understand him. I want to slap him and understand him and lick him and ignore him. I don't understand it. I don't understand myself anymore.

But I think I might care less about all of this once I've finished off this bottle of mediocre champagne.

THIRTEEN

Declan

THE BALLER EXPRESS

Maddie Cooper is fucking adorable and extra annoying when she's tipsy, and it just makes me want to punch a wall and kiss her.

She isn't trying to be adorable, but she *is* actively trying to annoy me. It's the easiest job in the world, trying to annoy me right now. That shitty stretch limo did it. All of Youngstown is doing it. This terrible hotel is definitely doing it. But Maddie Cooper is making a special effort, now that we're checked in, and for some reason it's *really* doing it for me.

How sad of a lonely sack of shit do you have to be to get turned on by a woman who's trying to annoy you?

"Are you going to call or at least text your family members to let them know we're in town?"

"Absolutely not, and I forbid you to contact them."

She doesn't even roll her eyes at my use of the term "forbid." That's how annoyed she is with *me* right now. And I'm not even *trying* to annoy her. "Why not?"

"Because I agreed to come for dinner on Christmas Eve. I did not agree to spend over twenty-four hours with them, and that is what would happen if they find out we're here. I'll be working in my room all night. If you would care to join me for whatever subpar in-room dining they have to offer here, then you may."

"No thanks."

"Fine."

"Great. Would you like me to order dinner to be served in your room?"

"Would you be ordering it as my girlfriend who's pretending to care about me or as my assistant who did not get us the adjoining rooms I requested?"

"I'd be ordering it as the woman who plans on eating dinner in the very nice hotel restaurant and wants to make sure you stay in your room so you don't ruin it for her." She sticks her tongue out at me. Actually sticks her tongue out at me, and it's somehow sexy and makes me want to impregnate her.

And it also makes me want to stay away from her because I'd just fuck everything up.

"I can order it myself, thanks. But don't you dare eat dinner by yourself in that dress."

That. Dress. That fucking sweater dress. Those fucking boots. Those fucking black tights or whatever you call those things that I can see through just a little bit and they make me want to rip them off her.

"I'm not going to hook up with anyone else while I'm with you here, Declan. But I am going to wear whatever I want, whenever I want to."

"Interesting choice of words."

She realizes she just said she isn't going to hook up with "anyone else" and turns a bewitching shade of pink. "You know what I mean."

"I always do, Cooper. Even when you don't."

"This building is so beautiful," she marvels, trying to change the subject.

"This is the ugliest carpet I've ever seen."

She shushes me. "Then don't look down." When I stab at the elevator call button, she pins me with a glare, lowering her voice. "Would you like me to see if I can find you last-minute accommodations at the YMCA? I seem to recall driving by one on the way here."

"You looked up alternate accommodations for me when you booked this place, didn't you?"

"I'm very thorough."

"You can't get rid of me that easily, girlfriend."

If she's smart, she'll try to. And I hope, for her sake, that she stays smart. Because I no longer trust myself around her.

The elevator dings and the doors open, and we step aside to let the elderly couple disembark, and then we get on the elevator together. I suppose my face must be doing something weird right now, because the old lady appears to be afraid of me—but that's just a misunderstanding. "Happy holidays!" I call out to them. And it's not my fault that I sounded a little too aggressive.

I press the button for our floor and wait for the doors to close and for a trapdoor in this car to open up and drop me into the fiery pit where I belong.

"You want to play with fire, you'd better be willing to get burned."

"By your terrible mood?"

"By the hot sting of my bare hand on your ass," I mutter.

Shit. Too far.

She meets my gaze in the reflection of the shiny brass doors in front of us and holds it for a fucking eternity, while I get all cozy here in the second circle of hell. "I don't seem to recall a separate spanking clause in our agreement, Mr. Cannavale."

Well, well. Now *the jingle hop has begun.*

Before I can even form another thought—I drop my bag, take her face in my hands, and kiss her.

Her lips are exactly as soft as they've threatened to be, and they part so readily for mine that I have to wonder if I'm dreaming. Both of our tongues taste like expensive mouthwash and cheap champagne and anticipation and dread. There's a moan and then a thud as she drops her bag to the floor too, and I feel her clinging to the lapels of my coat. I push her back against the wall. I don't remember if we're going up or down because I just want to go *in*, hard and deep.

The worst season ever just got awesome, and my hands are celebrating by sliding south to her waist, squeezing her sexy fucking hips. I pull that sweater dress up so my knee can rest there, snug between her legs, and she squeezes her thighs around it, rocking the night away. Good, naughty girl. Grunts and sighs and gasps echo around the elevator like the chorus of a dirty Christmas carol that we're both making up as we go along.

My hungry mouth finds her long, smooth neck, and I grab that tight bun on top of her head and tug on it so it comes apart, her dark hair cascading all around her, all around me. I want all of her to come apart for me like this. I want to spill every terrible thing that I am into her, every real part of myself that wants to be welcomed home. I need this right now, more than I need my dignity. I need this woman. This is all I want for Christmas.

My cock responds immediately to her throaty voice, but my brain is not registering a word she's saying.

My name, my name, my name is all I hear.

Maddie, Maddie, Maddie is all I'm thinking.

And then all I can feel is the hot sting of her bare hand on my face.

Chapter Fourteen

MADDIE: Declan. Answer your phone.
MADDIE: Oh for crying out loud. I'm sorry I slapped you. I'm so sorry. It was a reflex. Instinct.
MADDIE: I'm sorry if I hurt you. I'm really sorry. I panicked.
MADDIE: But you need to signal before changing lanes!
MADDIE: I mean, I guess I should have known what lane you're in. You haven't exactly been subtle. But there's a big difference between flirting and kissing. And you're just so damn slappable.
MADDIE: Declan. Open the door. We need to talk.
DECLAN: We don't need to talk. And you don't need to apologize. I'm not mad at you. I should not have done that. You should trust

your instincts. That was the right instinct. It won't happen again.
MADDIE: Declan. Now I feel bad.
MADDIE: It's not that I didn't like you kissing me. And touching me. And pulling on my hair. I just need a minute.
DECLAN: Trust me, you'd need a lot more than a minute to prepare yourself for what I'd do to you.
DECLAN: That probably sounded salacious, but I meant it in the other way. A warning. I appreciate that you came here with me. It means a lot. But it's best we stay away from each other until we have to go to my parents' house tomorrow.
DECLAN: Is that okay?
MADDIE: Just when I think you couldn't possibly find yet another way to be infuriating, you prove me wrong again.
DECLAN: I know it isn't fun, but you know I'm right about this. Good night, Cooper.

FIFTEEN

Declan

AWAY IN MY ANGER

EDDIE: Dude. When are you getting here? I'm pretty sure Nonna just served us a platter of deep-fried dog dicks.
EDDIE: They were pretty good though.
ME: <laughing face emoji> <dog emoji> <eggplant emoji> <Christmas tree emoji>
EDDIE: Are you drunk? Where are you? You're coming to dinner tomorrow, right?
ME: <thumbs up emoji> <thumbs up emoji> <thumbs up emoji>
EDDIE: When were you planning on telling me about your girlfriend?
ME: <smiling face with hearts emoji>
EDDIE: You're a dick.
ME: <raised middle finger emoji> When weren't you going for it you girls!

EDDIE: WHAT???
ME: Your girlfriend. You didn't tell my. Me. When.
EDDIE: Are you drunk right now, or are you having a stroke? Because either way, you haven't answered my question. When are you getting here?
ME: <raised middle finger emoji>
EDDIE: You ducking better be here tomorrow. Dick.

Yeah. I'm the dick. Declan Cannavale is the dick, everyone! Welcome to Dickville—population Me.

Corporate lawyers are easy targets.

Even when they totally aren't dicks.

Not really.

Would a dick order a Hot Toddy at a shitty hotel bar—three times?

"Another whiskey Hot Toddy, Rick," I say to the bartender, who may or may not be named Rick. But hey—sometimes people get mistaken for a dick, and sometimes they get mistaken for a Rick. "Hot Toddies for everyone!" I call out. "On me!" The pathetic crowd of about ten lame people cheers in a half-assed loser-y kind of way.

They certainly seem more excited to hear about the free Hot Toddies than they do the shitty band that's been playing shitty jazz versions of Christmas songs.

I'm having fun though. I'm having a great time. This is *exactly* how I pictured things going with Maddie once I'd gotten her away from the office, to a hotel in another city. I definitely did not plan to get her naked and fuck her fifty different ways into the New Year. Because that would have been wrong and bad. It would have been good and wrong, but it would have been bad in the very bad way. And she deserves better. "So damn slappable," she said. "Infuriating," she called me. I might be those things. Sometimes. To some people. But I'm also fun. I'm more fun than eating in a shitty hotel restaurant by yourself, that's for sure.

I check my phone again to confirm that she has continued to heed my warning to leave me alone.

She has. Good. *Now* she does what I ask her to do. Because I'm the Grinch who tries to make out with her in an elevator, and who'd want to hang out with that guy?

Except I'm fun. I am the axis around which all festive gatherings revolve. *I'll show her.*

I gulp down my Hot Toddy—fuck, I shouldn't have done that because it's hot—and then I hop off my seat at the bar. And I strut on over to the shitty little stage with all the swagger—swagger *and fun*—of a great entertainer. Because that's what I am. A fucking entertaining delight who's about to save Christmas for these pathetic losers in Whoville tonight.

The "singer" finishes the shitty song and says that

they're about to take a break, and that's when I step up and take the mic from her.

"Thanks, Shirley—let's hear it for Shirley and the band, everyone!" Her name might not be Shirley, but I usher Shirley off the stage and signal to the band to stay where they are. I tell them what to play next—because I'm the boss here—and say into the mic again, "Let's get this party started, Youngtown!"

I'm gonna jingle the fuck out of this Christmas carol. I'm gonna sing it like the badass crooner that I am, because *fuck you, Michael Bublé*. Dean Martin is better than you, and so am I!

"Dashing through the snow—sing it with me!
In a one-horse open sleigh
O'er the fields we go
Laughing all the way—because we're happy!
Bells on bobtails ring—what's a bobtail?
Making spirits bright—am I right?
What fun it is to ride and sing
A sleighing song tonight—we having fun yet?!
Jingle bells, jingle bells
Jingle all the way—can't hear you!
Oh, what fun it is to ride
In a one-horse open sleigh, hey
Jingle bells, jingle bells
Jingle all the way
Oh, what fun it is to ride
In a one-horse open sleigh."

I signal to the band to stop playing. "You know what—this is wrong. Stop! Nope. Fuck the happy songs. Not everyone is jingling all the way through the holidays, and they deserve to feel like they're a part of this too. Y'know? Because they aren't a part of anything else right now. If they were, they wouldn't be here in this shitty hotel bar. Who's feeling sad this Christmas? Show of hands." My hand, the one that's not holding the microphone, stays exactly where it is. Because I am not sad. Sad is for *other* people. Sad is for people who aren't fun or cool enough to be angry.

I see a couple of guys and one messy-haired drunk lady with their hands up. "Okay, good. Sad is good. Sad is real. Sad…is beautiful. Good for you—sad, lonely losers! Good for you! I'm gonna ask who else is angry next, okay, but sad people—this one's for you." I turn to the band and tell them what to play. "This is a song about a reliable little fir tree I like to call…Tannenbaum. We don't have enough songs about trees, you know that? Why is that? All songs should be about trees. All year long. Trees never break your heart. Trees don't wear sweater dresses and then slap you in the face when you're kissing them. Trees aren't a constant reminder of how little you have to offer them, even when you really, really want to give them…*something*…*anything*…any broken piece of you that they're willing to take… Fuck yeah, trees. This one's for all the sad people and all the awesome Tannenbaums out there who never make people sad."

SIXTEEN

Maddie

LUST CHRISTMAS

PIPER: Wait what?!?! OMG LOL SERIOUSLY?! You are in Ohio with Declan RN? I knew it! I knew you guys would HEA!!!
ME: Calm down. It's a work thing. Sort of. We are not a couple, and we are definitely not HEAing. Is that a verb now?
BEX: Wow. You called it, Piper! #MACLAN
PIPER: Wait. How did you know about Maclan, Mother? I never told you.
BEX: Um. You must have. How else would I know about it?
PIPER: Aunt Maddie please get me a safe for Christmas. Or let me move in with you kthx.
BEX: I totally do not read your fanfic Piper!!! When would I even have the time?!
PIPER: How would you even know that I write

fanfic if you weren't snooping in my room?! OH MY GAWD GET A LIFE, MOTHER! AND FYI I'M TOTALLY GETTING A SPECIAL LOCK FOR MY ROOM!!!!!
ME: Happy holidays, everyone! See you in a couple of days!
BEX: Oh sure. Go have hot sex with your hot boss in Ohio and leave me with the angry thirteen-year-old why don't you?
PIPER: Get a picture of his butt for me!!! Pretend he's a corporate ladder and climb him like a lady boss!!!
BEX: Piper!!!!!
ME: OMG Piper!!!
ME: Okay! Kiss the baby for me! Love you bye!

I mean, I'm *not* going to go have hot sex with my hot boss, but they wouldn't believe me if I'd told them that anyway.

I leave a generous tip for my waitress because it's a pretty slow night here at the Twinstar Hotel's restaurant. I actually got to do a little Kindle reading on my phone while I ate, so that was an unexpected benefit of this stupid trip. Not exactly worth getting up even earlier this morning to shave, but at least my hormones have normalized now. At least I'm no longer kicking myself for slapping Declan. At least I no longer want to slap him again for shutting me out.

We are clearly incompatible with each other, despite a...*significant* physical attraction and somewhat entertaining chemistry. And despite the fact that it was the hottest kiss of my life, and I basically had twelve orgasms when he squeezed my hips and shoved his knee between my legs and tugged on my hair and groaned in my ear and oh God I think I'm having another orgasm right now—despite all of that, he was right about one thing. We should stay away from each other until tomorrow.

I check my phone to make sure he hasn't changed his mind and sent me a booty-text.

Nope. Good. God forbid he should pester me or do anything inappropriate when I actually secretly want him to. He's probably in his room working, just like he said he would be. That elevator incident was probably just a blip on his radar. We're never on the same page. And that's that.

I'll go back to the room, take a bath, have a night cap while I watch a movie, and get a good night's sleep for a change. I'll enjoy the feel of my silky shaved legs against the clean hotel sheets, and I can spread out like a starfish because my boss's hot naked body won't be taking up any space at all under the covers.

I might just stop by his room and knock on the door one more time to see if he needs help with anything, work-wise. Since I'm here. And to see if he's shirtless in gray sweatpants, because I have a hunch he might be. Because gray sweatpants.

As I exit the restaurant and head to the bank of

elevators, I can hear someone singing the saddest version of "O Christmas Tree" I have ever heard. But I'm impressed by the smooth and rather depressing deep voice...and strangely aroused, as I head across the lobby to the bar.

When what to my wondering eyes do appear... But my hot boss and a band spreading holiday cheer.

Or running it over with a sad sexy sled, more like.

"*O Tannenbaum, O Christmas tree,*

Such pleasure do you bring me"

He croons into the mic with reckless melancholic abandon, barely recognizable as the cocky corporate lawyer I know and love to hate in Manhattan.

Oh God, I broke Declan Cannavale.

I take a seat at the bar and watch in horror along with the other dozen or so customers. Only, they don't seem to be horrified by his performance at all. They're mesmerized. And I am too. It's like Morrissey took a downer, put on a sexy sweater, and decided to do an impromptu show at some random bar in the Midwest. He's just as committed to this song as he is to being infuriating and to kissing me, and now my clitoris is going to tingle every time I see a fir tree until the end of time.

He seems to be getting more and more angry with each verse, though, and when he segues into "Silent Night," it's like every word is a curse word. The band keeps up with him, though. He seems to be completely unaware that I'm here, and that's probably a good thing.

Unfortunately, someone else is very aware that I'm here.

"Hello there" comes a male voice from right behind me.

Shit.

"Oh hello."

"What's a pretty woman like you doing alone at a bar tonight?"

"Just enjoying the entertainment," I tell him without taking my eyes off Declan.

"I'm Bryan," he says. "With a 'y.'" He holds his hand out for me to shake, which I do, but I still don't take my eyes off Declan. "What's your name?"

"It's Rey. Also with a 'y.'"

"Oh yeah? I've got an uncle named Ray. He isn't as good-looking as you are. I'm in town for business. Sales. What line of work are you in?"

"Me? I scavenge parts from ships and sell them."

"So we're both salespeople. I knew we'd have a connection."

Ugh, I can't talk to people who don't watch *Star Wars*.

Suddenly the singing stops, and I realize Declan has dropped the mic and is storming over here, his eyes fixed on Bryan "with a y." He gets right up in Bryan's very surprised face, towering over him, and stares him down.

"What do you think you're doing?" Declan hisses through gritted teeth.

"Uhh, I was just talking to my new friend Rey, here."

"Rey?" he says, turning to me, still frowning. "Rey?" He takes a deep breath and says in a deep, serious voice, "I want you to join me. We can rule together and bring a new order to the galaxy."

Shit. Declan Cannavale watches Star Wars. *Now I* really *can't hate him.*

"Don't do this, Ben," I quote flatly. "Please don't go this way."

"Hey man, I didn't realize you two were together. She didn't say anything."

"Oh, she didn't?" Now his wrath is entirely focused on me. "Interesting. Why's that, girlfriend?"

Bryan "with a y" quietly slinks away, unnoticed.

"I just hadn't gotten around to it yet."

Declan's arms are on either side of me, his hands gripping the edge of the counter that's pressing against my back. "Unacceptable," he mutters. He smells like whiskey and honey and so much testosterone. Seriously, I think his facial hair just grew half an inch while he was trying to intimidate Bryan.

"You're awfully uptight for a drunk *Star Wars* nerd."

"Seeing you with another guy sobered me up real fast. And my niece is obsessed with Rey Skywalker," he growls. "It's impossible to have a conversation with her without at least a passing understanding of the Galactic Republic, Rebel Alliance, and the Resistance."

"Sounds like my kinda girl. And you sound like a man who's memorized the *Star Wars* Wikipedia page."

He leans in even closer and whispers into my ear,

"I've also memorized all of the related Wikipedia sub-pages." He inhales my hair, and I'm sort of regretting that I don't have it up tonight so he can yank it down again. "What are you doing here, Maddie?"

"Well, I was enjoying the show. Do you take requests?"

"*You* obviously don't, because I requested that you stay away from me tonight."

"Technically, you're the one who didn't stay away from me, because I was sitting all the way across the room from you."

He straightens his arms, broadens his shoulders, and we're eye-to-eye again, and maybe, just maybe, we're finally on the same page. For now. And that page is straight out of my niece's fanfiction, I think, or more like the Kindle book I was reading at dinner. His nostrils are flaring. He's staring at my mouth. "You are always, always, always problematic, Cooper."

"Right back at you, Mr. Cannavale."

"Goddammit," he curses under his breath, his face slowly inching closer and closer to mine. He cradles my face with both hands, dragging the tip of his thumb across my lower lip. "Cooper," he whispers again, as if it's a curse word. "Cooper," he repeats, this time like a wish. And then he abruptly drops his hands, steps back, and walks away from me. Furiously dragging his fingers through his hair as he marches out of the bar, through the lobby. He's not marching in a perfectly straight line, but it's difficult to tell if that's due to the remaining alcohol in his system or the amazing thing in his pants that I felt against my leg.

And I can't believe the bastard is walking away from me.

Again.

Not tonight.

I march on after him. The lobby is empty. My heels click against the marble floor, and I can tell that Declan can hear me coming because his back straightens. Everything about that man is stiff, but he doesn't turn to face me.

I slip inside the elevator with him just as the doors are about to close. When he finally turns around, I push him against the wall of the elevator, cup my hands around the back of his neck, and bring him in for a kiss. A furious kiss. I let my lips and tongue tell him all the things I've already told him with words, but I've had it with words. I've had it with this man, and I've had it with not giving myself to him.

His hands are in my hair, and he meets my exasperated kisses with calm, controlled kisses that are even more maddening. He tugs on my hair, pulling my face away from his, and asks, "Have you been drinking?"

"You're going to drive me to drink even more if you stop kissing me right now."

"I want you to want this, Maddie."

"You're covered legally, now that I'm attempting to seduce you as predicted," I taunt. "What do you care?"

"Tell me you want me." The way he says it, it's an order, and for once, I am loving this bossy tone.

"I want you, Declan." He loosens his grip so I can lean in and take his earlobe between my teeth, tugging and then sucking on it, and then I whisper into his ear: "I want you to do and say every filthy thing you've ever wanted to do and say to me." The deep, guttural sound he makes is so satisfying. "And I'm going to do the same. To you."

His hands are on my hips now. "Fucking hell, I'm going to split you in two."

My hand slips to the glorious bulge in his pants. "Fuckin' A. I'm going to ride you like a one-horse open sleigh."

When the elevator doors open, he grabs my hand and pulls me down the hall, toward his room. "You should have let me walk away from you," he mutters.

"You should have let me into your room this afternoon. I would have really given you something to sing about."

"Oh, you already have. Believe me." He slides the key card through the slot, so aggressively, way too quickly. The light turns red. "Fuck." He does it again, with exactly as much force and speed. "*Fuck*."

"Let me do it."

"*I got it.*"

"No. You don't." I take the key card from him, slide it gently through the slot, and calmly hand it back to him. "Don't you dare be that gentle with *me* tonight."

He shoves the door open and pats me on the butt. "Get your ass in there, succubus. Now."

I hiss at him like a cat as I pass by him, throwing my purse into the room.

He stares me down, just like he did with whatshis-name at the bar.

When he shuts the door, he wastes no time tugging off his shoes and pulling his sweater off over his head, tossing everything to the floor. He is not wearing an undershirt. He is a God damn work of art.

Mentally, I am nodding and slow clapping like it's the end of an 80s teen underdog sports movie. But my body language is very convincingly telling him that I see this kind of thing all the time. I cross my arms in front of my chest and frown. "Wow. So you have a naked torso. What else ya got?"

SEVENTEEN

Declan

O COME, ALL YE FAITHFUL

Oh, I'll show you what else I got, Cooper.

I start unbuckling my belt. I'm still just inside the door of this terrible hotel room, and she's backlit by the horrible lamps, but she's so fucking beautiful and so fucking aggravating. Standing there, with her arms crossed in front of that chest. She did as I told her to and changed out of that wicked sweater dress, but she's still wearing those black tights and those black high-heeled boots.

"What is that you're wearing?" I ask as I let my pants drop to the floor.

The widening eyes and the gasp, as she gets a preview of what I've got, is so satisfying, but I keep my boxer briefs on. She's going to have to wait to see the goods.

She smooths down the front of that dress, clearing her throat. "It's a wrap dress."

"That's the kind of dress my granny wears," I say as I close the distance between us. Because I can't go one more second without touching her. "How do you look hot in this?" I trace the edge of the deep V neckline with my fingertip, from her collarbone, all the way down. She shivers, and that is also satisfying.

"I look even hotter out of it." She says it like it's a dare. As if I didn't already have big plans for getting her out of it. As if I'm not constantly picturing her naked, no matter what she's wearing.

"Devil woman." I graze my palms across her hard nipples as I reach down to grip the sides of her dress, kissing her once, and then pull the thing off over her head in one swift motion. And God damn. *God. Damn.* She does look even hotter out of it.

That fucking black lacy bra. Those fucking black lace panties under those fucking see-through tights. All that smooth skin. All those evil curves. I don't have an artistic bone in my body, but I want to stick a rose stem in her mouth and then paint and sculpt her. I want to write a cheesy love song about those spectacular tits.

"Are you going to stare at me all night, or are you actually going to do something interesting for a change?"

That fucking mouth.

There's that hint of Staten Island again.

I back her up two steps, to the dresser, so she has something to grab on to because she'll need it. I get a good grip on the waistband of her tights and rip those fuckers apart as I drop to my knees before her. Satisfying doesn't even begin to describe how it feels when they actually come apart, tearing down the middle and along the insides of her creamy white thighs.

"Was that really necessary?" she asks—her voice, everything trembling.

"No. But it was fucking awesome."

Merry fucking Christmas to me!

I squeeze her ass and blow warm breath over her clit through the lace. Her arousal is evident, even before I touch her between her legs. She squeezes her thighs together so tight. I will never be able to torment her as thoroughly as she has tormented me for two months, but I will have a jolly old Saint Nick of a time trying. With the pad of one thumb, I massage her clit in small, firm circles, and she is so wet for me I could cry.

She's whimpering, trembling harder now, trying to keep it together. But I know what the anticipation is doing to her. I know what it's doing to me. And I know exactly how much longer I can go without being inside her, and it's not very long.

I push the black lacy triangle of her panties to the side, and *fuck me under the mistletoe*, she's shaved bare as the North Pole and this is the best Christmas present anyone has ever given me.

"You are a devious, wonderful woman."

"I know." She raises one leg to rest the back of her knee on my shoulder. She makes the heel of her boot dig into my back for a second, and I like it. Naughty girl.

I punish her with my tongue.

I thank her with my fingers.

I worship her with my mouth.

She serenades me with sweet, heavenly sighs and moans and curses that would make a drill sergeant blush.

I decide to serenade her a little with my Irish tongue again, see if it has any effect this time. "You're a feckin' stunner, Maddie Cooper, and your fanny tastes like heaven. I'd feast on you for breakfast, lunch, and dinner."

She tenses up, shivers, and goes limp for a second.

Feck yeah, Irish.

"Devil tongue," I think she mumbles.

One of her hands is in my hair, tugging and combing, and I would stay here like this for half an hour if it were the second or third time I'd had her. But it's the first. I won't let it be the only. I will take her as many ways as I can tonight, as soon as I make her come once or twice right now.

Lazy swirling, rapid fluttering, determined flicking, relentless tongue-fucking, and well-timed clit sucking does the job efficiently and effectively. She surrenders to me, and we are both rewarded with her shudders and rhythmic contractions, convulsing as she groans and frantically cries out. A dirty, delectable fallen angel.

I don't know what it is about this woman that makes me extra Catholic, but *I believe, I believe, I believe.*

When she is limp and sighing, I stand up and carry her with me to deposit her onto the massive bed. I do not regret not being gentle, because she bounces magnificently, and she knows it. She smirks at me, lies back on her elbows, and lifts her foot up to rest on my chest. I unzip her boots, pulling them off, one by one, tug off what's left of those black tights.

I'm about to slip those black panties down her legs when she pulls back and sits up on her knees. She reaches behind herself, staring up at me. I take in a sharp breath because I know I'm about to hold it for a really long time, and *Good King Wenceslas,* she slowly removes the lacy bra and then tosses it at me. I catch it and clutch it to my heart before discarding it. I see stars and hear harp music, and it's *sexy* harp music. My cock feels as big and lit up as the Rockefeller Center Christmas tree.

"Fucking hell, Maddie," I manage on an exhale.

Her eyelids flutter and I know it's because I called her by her first name.

"Maddie," I repeat, crawling toward her.

She backs away from me, dragging herself up to the pillows. She has a smug expression on her face now, emboldened by the unbridled lust in my eyes, I'm sure. She spreads her arms out along the top of the headboard, lifting herself up. When I reach her, I bury my face in her glorious breasts. I emit some sad, not-at-all-cool sound from the back of my throat, but I swear I've never been this happy. My hands are all over her, exploring her, claiming her. My mouth is all over her, savoring the taste of her warm skin and hungry for something that I haven't even let myself fantasize about with her.

She's straddling me now, bearing down on me and

rocking back and forth. Just when I thought she couldn't possibly find another way to infuriate me, she proves me wrong. And I like it.

I feel like a sex-starved sixteen-year-old virgin, but I'm performing like a man. I know this because I'm making her come again just from licking and sucking. She's saying my name and *Oh God, oh shit, oh fuck* over and over again. She's breathless and amazed and kind of angry—like *how dare you make me feel this good?*—and it's so hot.

She lifts herself up a bit and slides one hand down my chest, into my boxer briefs. She strokes the underside of my shaft, gently a few times, up and down, teasing the sensitive spot beneath the head. Carefully, she reaches down again to pay tribute to a part of me that not enough women have tended to in my life—and all I want for Christmas is *this*. And then she sucks in her breath when she takes hold of me. The firm grip and warmth of her soft hand on the heat of my hard cock, the way she peeks down for a look, biting her lower lip. She's a naughty girl, and she wants me.

"Get over yourself," she says when she sees me smirking at her.

"Oh, I have. I'm used to how amazing I am. I'll just give *you* a minute to get comfortable with it."

Before she can give me a snarky comeback, I drag my fingernails down her back—with just the right amount of pressure—and give her a quick smack on the ass. That shudder and gasp tells me she wants another one, and I give it to her.

But then I'm back to her tits because I need to

make sure they know how much I care about them. I care about them with my hands, and I care about them with my mouth. I care about the left one, and I care about the right one, and I don't have a favorite. They're both the best.

I'm moaning and she's groaning, and we sound so good together.

I will devour this woman. I could lose myself in this woman, find myself again… But then what?

She senses my apprehension all of a sudden and places her hands on either side of my face. She is returning from her state of ecstasy to check on me. Her eyes are hooded but kind. That combination of genuine concern and desire is what will do me in. I close my eyes and feel her kiss me, gently, on my forehead and then whisper in my ear, "No thinking tonight, Mr. Cannavale. It's just my body and your body… And us being straightforward and moderately rational when it comes to sex… We will not let this interfere with our fantastic work relationship, *come what may.*"

God, I love it when she repeats my brilliant words back to me. I open my eyes and see her grinning at me. "*'Come what may?'* Exactly how drunk are you right now?"

"Exactly drunk enough to demand that you fuck me immediately…*sir.*"

"Yes, ma'am."

EIGHTEEN

Maddie

WE CAME UPON A MIDNIGHT CLEAR

Sweet baby Jesus, it's happening.

Peace on Earth, good will to my vagina, Hallelujah, for the love of Josh Groban and all things holy, it is finally happening.

I had forgotten that I got a little too enthusiastic while shaving this morning. I was afraid I looked like one of those hairless cats down there, but Declan really seems to like it, and I've already had more orgasms in half an hour than I ever had with any of my exes, so I must like it too. Or maybe my body just really likes Declan's body. Because we're both hot as fuck and also both so good at knowing that sometimes sex is just sex. Sometimes amazing sex is just amazing sex. And sometimes your blazing hot boss goes to town on your lady bits like he's competing in the all-new Winter Olympics sport of Tongue Gymnastics.

And he is the world champion. He wins all the gold medals.

He is also very graciously giving me the honor of doing the unveiling of his trophy. I carefully peel the elastic waistband away from his taut, golden skin, and I actually do want to sing a hymn in tribute to this thing. I hate to mix metaphors, but it's going to be like trying to fit a Costco-sized bottle of champagne into a tiny Manhattan apartment-sized cupboard. I am nervous but also determined. And very, very lubricated. And ready to celebrate making Declan pop his cork.

I swipe the condom package from his fingers.

"I didn't ask you to assist me with that," he chastises.

"I'm good at this."

"You need to get better at taking orders."

"Maybe *you* need to get better at giving them."

I finish rolling the condom onto the impossibly hard length of his erection and then look up at him, my mouth watering. His jaw is so tight. All of his muscles are flexed and ready for action. His whole body is so tense and agonizingly beautiful, his heated gaze is so intense—I almost lose my nerve… Almost.

"Lie down on your back, Maddie," he growls. "Now."

I do as he says, resting my head on the pillow and straightening my legs out on either side of him.

He hovers over me, holding himself up with one hand, positioning his cock with the other. "I want you to tell me exactly how it feels to have me inside you. Tell me what you want. Understand?"

"Yes."

He teases my entrance with the tip. "You ready?"

"Yes."

"I don't think you are."

"I want it."

"You want me?"

"I want you inside me."

He eases into me. Slowly, slowly.

I gasp. "Oh my God."

"You're so fucking tight."

"You're so big and it stings, but I'm so wet for you."

"You are. So wet. You okay?"

"Yes. More."

He gives me more. Inch by infuriating inch. He whispers on an exhale, "Babyyyyy."

I slowly bend my legs, tilt my hips, wrap my legs around him. I have to touch his face, feel his stubble on the skin of my fingertips. Kiss his cheek and kiss his open mouth and lick his chin because he's delicious. "Oh God, I like it. I like how you fill me up."

"It feels so good."

"Yes. More." I don't even know who this man is to me anymore except the man who's fucking me and making me feel better than anyone has ever made me feel. He pushes in more, and I jerk up, arching my back, crying out. "Oh God! It hurts, and it's good." I wrap my arms around his back so tight and then drag my fingernails across his skin, the way he did to me and it surprised me and I liked it. "Shit. Declan. Stay inside me. Just move and stay inside me," I plead.

He sucks in a breath and starts rocking into me. My hips match his movements. I accommodate him, and it feels so right, and I'm so mad that we haven't done this before. I place my feet flat on the mattress so I can move my hips more. He groans, and I remember to tell him how I feel and what I want. "I'm so fucking mad at you for not fucking me sooner."

"Me too."

"Goddammit, this feels better than anything."

He grunts.

"Fuck me harder."

He grunts again, and then he fucks me harder. I reach back for the headboard for leverage.

"Give me everything," I manage to squeak out.

"I don't think you can handle it," he mutters.

"Try me."

I look down at him just once and see the vein in the side of his neck, and then I close my eyes because good Lord, he's going deeper and moving faster and giving me everything, and I can handle it. I can and I can't. I just want it. I want him, and I've never known this kind of want before.

He's working so hard, giving me what I asked for.

I couldn't handle hearing him call me Maddie before, but now I need to hear him say my name. "Declan," I whisper.

His reply is another grunt.

He's ramming into me so hard, I can't hold on to

the headboard anymore. My hands slip and my arms spread out to the side, and he doesn't even look up, but his hand shoots up between the crown of my head and the headboard to protect me. Lightning reflexes. Good heart. I just fell a little bit in love with Declan Cannavale, and I don't even care because he deserves it.

We're both slick with sweat now. I press my tits up so he can feel them against his chest as he moves. "Fuck. Maddie." He groans.

I take his face in my hands again, his stubble softer now from sweat, and I kiss his mouth again, ravenous. He slows his thrusts so I can suck on his tongue. So I can lick his stubbly sexy face. His lips find mine, and he kisses me forcefully. Grabs hold of my hands and holds them over my head. I'm making high-pitched whimpering sounds that I've never made before in my life. I want him to stay inside me, and I want to kiss him forever, but this was supposed to be a quick angry hate fuck.

He kisses my neck, licks me all the way from my cleavage up to my chin, and then devours my mouth with his. Our tongues can't get deep enough inside each other's mouths. He jerks his head back suddenly, dips his head down to kiss my breasts. He's so hungry for me, and I want to give all of myself to him. Feed myself to him.

I wrench my wrists free from his grip so I can grab his ass and tilt my pelvis up, wrapping my legs around him again. We're panting and gasping for air, but I feel like I can finally breathe around him. Like this is the most honest I've ever been since I met him.

My hands slide up the length of his torso and into his hair. He's so deep inside me, and my whole body is full of him and tingling all over, and I think I might actually be happy. I kiss his ear, his neck, his shoulder. I would kiss him everywhere right now if I could.

Just as I've relaxed completely into the rhythm of his thrusts, he lifts me up so he's sitting and I'm straddling him. He kisses and squeezes my breasts, so eager but masterful. Just like before, except he's inside me now. I rock back and forth and bear down on him. Waves of pleasure take over. His mouth all over me, his cock inside me, his hands on my hips now. I arch my back, reach for the mattress, offering myself to him. He's so blind with lust, and I still can't give him enough.

This was supposed to be hard and fast, some wicked voice echoes through my head.

But that voice gets muffled by the one that's crying out "Oh my God! Declan! Declan! Yes!"

He starts thrusting up into me, so hard and fast, and the dull pain is divine.

Infuriating.

Totally satisfying.

And then he pulls out and it's devastating. He flips me around onto my hands and knees, grabs on to my shoulder with one hand, my waist with the other, and thrusts relentlessly. It's pure animal lust, and it's fucking beautiful because it's all for me.

"Maddie." His throat is constricted. He's so close

to the edge, and he's waiting for my permission to go over, and I fall in love with him just a little more.

I can give him what he needs right now, and I want to. "No one's ever fucked me this good, Declan. Never, ever."

There. Best gift ever. Just for him.

He makes the most beautiful guttural noise, and just when I think it's all for him now, he grabs a fistful of my hair and tugs on it, and I come again. Sharply. Unexpectedly. He slams into me and then wraps his arm around my waist and pulls me to him, holding me tight.

I wish I could see his face.

And then I have the craziest wish I've ever had—that he could just come inside me.

But that really is crazy.

When he's completely still, and he's exhaled all the breath, I let myself fall forward and bring him with me.

He's still inside me, still half-hard.

He lies flat on my back.

He wraps both arms around my waist.

He kisses my upper back, and then I feel his soft, damp, stubbly cheek against it.

As if he knows how much I love the way it feels, he rubs his cheek into my skin.

"Fuck" is all he says.

And then he doesn't say anything, and I know he's asleep.

My cheek is flat against the pillow, but I'm not moving.

My head is still spinning, and my body is still tingling, and we lie like this for a minute maybe, and I swear I can already feel Declan stirring inside me.

This was supposed to be fast. This was supposed to be furious.

I have a feeling it *will* be, for Round Two, but this first time… This first time with Declan was more. It was more, and it was just the beginning, and I'm not even scared right now because it was so good. And we both deserve to feel good. Even if it's with each other.

Even if it won't last.

Maybe even if it will.

NINETEEN

Declan

O HOLY SHIT

What's the actual last thing you'd ever want your executive assistant to see you doing the morning after you had hot drunk, angry sex with her in a terrible hotel room? Dancing around your terrible hotel room to "Come and Get Your Love" like Star-Lord in *Guardians of the Galaxy*—naked? Yeah. Me too.

And yet, here we are.

My damp, naked self and my assistant and some lady in a pantsuit.

"Um. You weren't answering your phones or the door," Maddie says, her face tense because she's trying so hard not to laugh. "So I was worried you had passed out or something… This is Karen. She works for the hotel. She let me in."

"Hi, Karen," I mutter through gritted teeth. There's no point in side-stepping back to the bathroom because they can't unsee what they just saw.

Karen finally manages to tear her bulging eyes away from the general area that I'm covering with my hands. "Hi... Um. We're very pleased to have you here at The Twinstar, Mr. Cannavale. I actually heard you singing at the bar last night, and I really enjoyed it. You have a really great voice."

"Fantastic. Thanks."

"Thank you for your help, Karen." Maddie gives her a wide-eyed toothy grin. "That will be all."

"Right." Karen takes one last look at my big sexy hands over my big sexy junk before turning away and waving. "Let me know if there's anything else I can—"

"Thank you, *Karen*!" Maddie and I both yell out at the same time.

Karen nods and says, "Happy holidays!" as she exits the room, shutting the door behind her.

Now I'm alone with the succubus. I woke up after noon, thinking last night might have been a dream. A really long, incredibly realistic, filthy sex dream. Because I woke up alone in my bed, with rumpled sheets and the heavenly scent of Maddie Cooper's magical pussy all over them. Only I didn't feel depleted. I felt energized. I felt happier than I've felt all year.

Which is why I was listening to the radio while I was in the shower. Which is why I was singing and dancing around to "Come and Get Your Love" while I was in the shower. And why I continued singing and dancing around to "Come and Get Your Love" after I had gotten out of the shower. Because I thought I was alone. And I was happy.

And now, *this*.

She's fully dressed in a nice pair of jeans and a tight sweater, and it is very fitting that I am standing naked before her. Although, I feel less naked now than I did at certain times last night. And I'm not talking about how I was physically naked when I was coming in her mouth or when I was growling "You like that don't you, dirty girl?" when I was balls deep or when I was literally fucking her sideways on the sofa. I'm talking about how good it felt to call her "babyyyy" when I was pressing myself inside her for the first time. I'm talking about how it felt like my heart might burst—not because I was fucking her like a raging bull but because she was stroking and kissing my face like she needed it as much as I did. I'm talking about all the times I had to hold my breath just to keep from blurting out "I love you" when I was coming, because it felt more like love than anything I've felt in years.

Maybe ever.

And I swear, she was kissing me harder and deeper, just to keep herself from saying it too.

But if she's thinking about any of those things we did and said and didn't say last night, she isn't revealing it on her annoyingly fresh and smirky face right now.

She clears her throat. "Can I get you a towel?"

"I can get one myself, thanks."

"Are you sure?"

"Yes."

"Are you going to do it anytime soon?"

"Are you going to just stand there staring at me forever, or is there a particular reason you were trying to get ahold of me?"

"I've been texting and calling you all morning."

I'm finally realizing I don't even know where my phone is. The one person I've always wanted to call or text for the past two months was with me, so I didn't give a shit where my phone was. Maddie looks around, sees my pants from last night on the floor, and pulls my phone out of one of the pockets.

"You'd better charge it," she says, holding the phone out to me.

I don't reach for it because I'm still covering my junk.

"Feeling shy this morning?" she coos. And then she spots the charger on my dresser and plugs it in for me without my asking.

"I'm feeling a number of things at the moment. Shy isn't one of them."

She meets my gaze through the reflection in the mirror above the dresser, sucking in her breath. She doesn't say a thing.

So that's how it's gonna be.

I run both hands through my hair and go back to the bathroom to turn off the radio and towel myself off. Yeah, I made sure she was watching me in the mirror when I did it. No, I'm not expecting her to join me in here. Yes, we need to get into holiday family mode. Also *yes*, I have every intention of jingling her bells again later tonight.

When I stroll back out to get dressed, I've got a bath towel wrapped around my waist and Maddie's leaning against the dresser. She's fidgeting, and I'm glad. When she sees me, her gaze sweeps down the length of me, and she reaches back to steady herself. I'm really fucking pleased about it because I was beginning to think she'd become immune to me.

I proceed to get dressed. I had already laid my clothes out on the bed. I can feel her eyes on me, and I can feel how nervous she is right now.

"So, your whole family knows I'm coming, yes?"

"Yes. They're looking forward to meeting you. You don't have to be nervous."

"Believe it or not, I'm always a little nervous when I meet my boyfriends' families for the first time."

It is totally irrational, how I am seized with jealousy at the notion of her meeting the families of her other boyfriends. Of her "real" boyfriends.

"Exactly how many boyfriends' families have you met, exactly?"

"Only five. And, I mean, two of those boyfriends were from high school, so I really only met them because we didn't have our drivers licenses yet and needed a ride."

"And the other three? They were serious?"

"No." She looks down at the floor. "I wouldn't categorize them as serious."

"Then why'd you meet their families?"

She shrugs. "I think they wanted to impress their parents, to be honest." She laughs. "They were kind of deadbeats. I had a good job. Y'know. I'm sure their parents would have preferred they got better jobs, but at least I won them a few points."

"I get that," I deadpan. "I hope mine finally get off my back for not becoming a surgeon."

She smiles, shaking her head. "This is so crazy."

"What is?"

"Me pretending to be your girlfriend." She watches me for a response.

I finish buttoning up my shirt. "Why?"

She shrugs again. She seems so vulnerable all of a sudden, and it's killing me just a little. "Am I dressed okay? I forgot to ask if it's going to be casual or formal, or…"

I walk over to her, tilt her chin up, and kiss her, just once, lightly on the mouth. As soon as I do, her hands go to my waist and she rests her forehead against my chest. She isn't wearing heels, for once, and she seems a lot smaller today. I kiss the top of her head and wrap my arms around her shoulders. "I had a great time last night."

"Me too."

"I want to do that again."

She laughs. "Which part?"

"Definitely the beginning part. And the thing on the sofa. And the part where I made you come just from kissing your—"

"Okay, okay. Let's not get too detailed right before going to your family thing."

She gives me a little pat on the ass, and I can tell she isn't nervous anymore.

"It's casual," I tell her. "But I'd advise against wearing tight jeans."

"Why?"

"Because you'll be eating. A lot."

"These aren't all that tight," she says, sticking her fingers between the waist of her jeans and her belly. "There's a little room to grow."

"You're gonna need a lot more room than that. Did you bring sweatpants? A tracksuit?"

She scoffs. "You're wearing regular pants."

"These are one size up, can't you tell? I'm wearing a belt, which I will be loosening throughout the day. Put on a stretchy dress or something."

"I don't want to wear a dress if everyone else is casual."

This is such a relationship-y conversation, and it's making me really happy again. "Okay. Wear whatever you feel comfortable in. But don't say I didn't warn you." I give her hips a little squeeze before going back over to the bed to finish getting ready.

"Advice noted, thanks. I ordered a cab to pick us up in an hour. You didn't eat breakfast, did you?"

"No. Did you?"

"Yeah. I ordered room service. Is that okay?"

"You could have ordered it in here. With me."

She twists her lips to the side. "It didn't seem like a good idea."

"As opposed to what we did last night?" I raise my eyebrows at her and then waggle them.

She crosses her arms in front of her chest. "I don't recall a discussion or detailed written description of the extent of this discreet, temporary simulated consensual romantic relationship."

I put my jacket on and cross my arms in front of my chest too. "Let's negotiate right now. Shared meals in private—in bed or out of it—are on the table."

"Agreed. Private serenading of Christmas carols—on the table."

"Enh. I've heard you sing, and I'm going to have to pass."

"Screw you."

"Absolutely. On the table… Under the table…"

Eye roll. "Naked dance parties—on the table."

"Agreed."

"Christmas presents are off the table."

"Unacceptable."

"It's too much pressure. There will be no exchanging of Christmas gifts."

"Fine."

"Sleepovers are off the table."

"Disagree. Convince me otherwise."

She starts to say something and then snaps her mouth shut. Her eyes are a little watery, and she looks so vulnerable again. And I'm falling for her again, just a little.

"I just don't think we should, Declan. You know why."

I do. I know why, and I want her in my bed all night anyway. But I don't want her to feel vulnerable. "Yeah. Agreed."

There's a flash of something in her eyes, and it may be disappointment. But she nods once and sighs.

"Great. Guess that covers everything, right? Probably not necessary to mention, however—butt stuff—off the table."

I hold a hand up to protest.

"Let's just get through Christmas Eve dinner and revisit this later."

I sigh and lower my hand. "Agreed."

"So how many other girlfriends have you introduced to your family?" she asks with a sing-song voice. So innocent. So unaware.

And I'm finally going to have to make her aware of the thing that I haven't wanted to talk about, with her or anyone else.

"Just one," I tell her. "Just one."

Chapter Twenty

DECLAN: Where are you?
DECLAN: Maddie. Seriously. Are you in your room? Open the door.
DECLAN: You can't just leave like that. Are you still coming to my parents' house or not?
MADDIE: Calm down. I'm in the lobby gift shop.
DECLAN: Why?
MADDIE: Because I need to bring a gift for your parents.
DECLAN: They won't expect one. Trust me. You don't have to do that.
MADDIE: I need to bring something for your parents.
MADDIE: And I need to be alone so I can process this. I can't believe you dropped this bomb on me right before I meet everyone.
DECLAN: My dad taught all of us to swim by dropping us into a pool. But he was always

right there to make sure we didn't drown. I'm here if you want to talk. But I've known about it for half a year, and being alone all that time hasn't helped me to process it. At all.
MADDIE: Declan. I'm really sorry that your significant ex is marrying your brother. I'm sad for you. I don't want to make this all about me. BUT YOU SHOULD HAVE TOLD ME ABOUT THIS WHEN YOU ASKED ME TO COME WITH YOU AND YOU SHOULD HAVE TOLD ME THEY'D BE THERE TODAY WTF IS WRONG WITH YOU???!!! <face with rolling eyes emoji> <swearing face emoji> <woman face-palming emoji>
MADDIE: Sorry for text-yelling. This is why I didn't want to be in the same room with you.
DECLAN: I didn't tell you because I didn't want you to think it would be a shitty stressful occasion. I mean, all family holiday dinners are, but I didn't want you to worry about it.
MADDIE: Thanks for dropping me in the deep end of the pool with no floaties, boss.
DECLAN: Anytime, Cooper. Always looking for fresh new ways to infuriate you.
MADDIE: Okay, I know it's dumb to ask you this in a text. But I don't think I can handle seeing your face right now… Are you still in love with her? With Hannah?
DECLAN: No. I'm not, Maddie. We were off and on for the last few years. I got her to move out to New York with me a year and a half

ago. She broke up with me after last Christmas and moved home because I didn't spend enough time with her.
MADDIE: When was the last time you talked to her or your brother?
DECLAN: Haven't talked to Brady since he called to tell me they were engaged. Around half a year ago. Haven't talked to her since I found out.
MADDIE: Did she try to get in touch with you?
DECLAN: Yes.
MADDIE: Declan! So you're still mad at both of them? Are you going to make a scene?
DECLAN: I don't make scenes, Cooper. I solve problems. Sometimes I solve problems by avoiding them. I know this may shock you, but I'm not perfect. And I'm not as mad about anything when I'm with you. Which is why I wanted you around. Sorry if that was selfish of me.
DECLAN: Anything else?
MADDIE: <crying face emoji> Everything else, Declan. Everything else. Also, do you think your parents would like a pair of shot glasses with the Cleveland skyline etched onto them? They're sort of pretty.
DECLAN: I'm coming downstairs to kiss you now. <nerd face emoji>

TWENTY-ONE

Declan

HAVE A JOLLY CANNAVALE CHRISTMAS

"You grew up in this house?" Maddie asks as the cab drives off and we walk, hand-in-hand, up the long driveway.

They've got the usual Christmas lights up. Clear white around the roof because my nonna insists colored lights are ostentatious. Colored lights around the covered porch because my ma thinks white lights are boring. It doesn't look like Aiden and Brady are here yet, so I breathe easier. "Yeah. They don't need a house this big anymore, but my dad refuses to move."

"Stubborn?"

"Secretly sentimental, I think."

I can feel her soft gaze on me as I stare up at the house.

She squeezes my hand, reassuring me when I'm the one who should be reassuring *her*. I'm an asshole for not telling her about Brady and Hannah sooner, but I didn't want her to come because she felt sorry for me. I just wanted her to be here. With me.

"It's a nice house," she says. "Seems like a nice, quiet neighborhood."

"Yeah, well. We'll see how you feel about that when you're inside with my family."

She guffaws. "You clearly have never been to Christmas dinner with my extended family on Staten Island. Or dinner with my family on any night, anywhere."

I really want that. I want to have dinner with her family on Staten Island or anywhere. But I don't think that's on the table.

We walk up the steps of the front porch and stand in front of the door. I can hear Dean Martin blaring from the speakers in the living room—the only acceptable singer of Christmas songs in the Cannavale house because he was an Italian-American from Ohio. I can hear my ma yelling at my dad about something. I look down at Maddie, who's straightening her coat and fidgeting with her gift bags. "They aren't here yet. You ready?"

"Yep. Let's do this."

I ring the doorbell. I have a key, but I'm hoping my ma will stop yelling if she knows we're out here.

"It's on the top shelf!" she bellows. "Tony! No—the middle top shelf!"

No such luck.

The door flies open, and I already know from the look on her beautiful face that they somehow found out that I was in town yesterday and didn't tell them.

Fuck. And now I just have to wait for someone to bring it up.

"Awww, there's my beautiful boy" is what she says though. "And who's this beautiful lady? Come in, get inside! It's colder than your nonna's icy black heart out there." She ushers us in, closing the door behind us while yelling at my dad. "Casey and them are in the family room watching a movie. Eddie's here, Nonna's in the kitchen of course, but no one else yet." She clears her throat.

The living and dining room are decorated exactly like they are every year. I can see the Rudolph ornament I made when I was seven hanging on the fake white tree. My old stocking is hanging from the mantle, in between Casey's and Eddie's as always, and it *isn't* filled with coal. I take a deep breath because I'm home, and I'm actually happy about it. But I feel more at home now than I have in years, and I wasn't expecting that. I finally let go of Maddie's hand to hug Ma. And then I watch these two women hug each other, and it's pretty great. I'm way too much of a badass to tear up, but if I were ever going to tear up, it would be right this second.

The air in the house isn't smoky exactly, but it's thick with the aroma of several gallons of boiling hot cooking oil, seven kinds of seafood, tomatoes, basil, parmesan cheese, and four decades worth of unspoken cultural and personal tension between my Irish-American Ma and Nonna. But in a good way. And every now and then you get a whiff of all the sugary deep-fried dough as a reminder of the sweeter things to come if you can survive dinner and make it to dessert.

Tonight, I need to not only make it to dessert but back to the hotel and Maddie Cooper's delicious pussy.

But I can't think about that right now.

"Hiya, Maddie—welcome to our humble home. My name's Mary Margaret, but you can call me Mamie."

"You have a lovely home," Maddie says, holding up one of the gift bags. "Merry Christmas. Here's just a little something from the hotel gift shop. I'm so sorry I didn't have time to go shopping before we left New York."

"Ohhhh! Lookie lookie!" She tears into it immediately and holds up the Cleveland, Ohio tea towel and a Cleveland souvenir Christmas tree ornament. "Aww, so sweet. We never get to enjoy this kind of thing since we live here." Maddie gets her cheek pinched. "Thank you, hon. Thought that counts. Let's get your coats off. Tony! Dec and his girl are here!" she yells out. "That man, I swear. I hope my son is giving you less grief than my husband gives me."

"Oh, he's a real prince," Maddie says, almost convincingly.

I take Maddie's coat and hang both of ours up on the coat rack by the door.

My dad yells out from the kitchen, and it's a wonder we can hear him over Dean Martin, but he's got quite the voice. "You want me to find the platter, or you want me to come out and see the guests?!"

"I'll get the platter!" she yells.

That's when my favorite niece comes bounding in, followed by my sister. Casey is probably more relieved than anyone that I have a new girlfriend, because that means she won't have to break up any fights tonight. Probably.

"Uncle Dec!" Penelope's holding up the Rey Deluxe Lightsaber that I sent her. "Uncle Dec! I opened it already, look!"

"Hey there, Wookie."

She jumps up into my arms, still holding the toy weapon. "I'm not a Wookie, I'm a Jedi."

"Oh, that's right. Have you been a good Jedi this year? Or did you switch to the dark side?"

I speak fluent *Star Wars* Nerd with my niece while watching Casey chat with Maddie and my ma and realize that all four of my favorite girls are in this room with me right now, and this is probably going to be the high point of the night.

It's over as soon as my dad walks in, sighing loudly as if it's such a burden to have to greet guests in his house when he'd rather be at a local football game in the freezing cold.

"There he is," he says. "Finally gracing us with his presence."

I let Penelope slide down the side of me and go over to Casey so she can introduce her to Maddie. Casey mouths to me from across the room, *I love her!* and gives me a thumbs-up.

"Merry Christmas," I say to my dad, holding my hand out to shake his. His hair's a little grayer than it was the last time I saw him, but Tony Cannavale still looks like a cross between Tony Soprano and Cake Boss. Except he's Ohio-born and bred. And he's never had anyone killed or baked anything in his life. As far as I know.

He gives my hand an abrupt shake while patting my shoulder. "You know I got friends all over town, right? I got a buddy, his nephew went to school with you—few years younger—says he saw you at the Twinstar last night. Singing in the hotel bar." He gives me a somewhat gentle smack up the side of my head. "You're in town yesterday, and you don't give your ma a phone call? Not even a quick hello? What's the matter with you?"

"Come meet Maddie, ya big oaf," my ma says to him. "Aw, my boy doesn't need to call his ma. I'm sure he knew how busy I was gettin' the house ready for guests and cleanin' up after your mother in the kitchen and gettin' ready for all the *everything*…" Ma comes over to pinch my cheek—really hard. "I mean, what's he gonna do—stop by to see us for half an hour when he's ten whole minutes away? Nahhh."

"Actually—it wasn't his fault, Mr. and Mrs. Cannavale," Maddie offers. "I wasn't feeling well when we got in yesterday. I really hate flying. So I was resting, and he didn't want to leave me alone."

Fuck me, I want to put a little Christmas bun in that oven right now.

"Awww. That sounds like Mr. Bigshot, all right. Doesn't want to leave the hotel his sick girlfriend is in, but he'll go down to the bar to get drunk and sing to a bunch of strangers."

"Hey—I wasn't *that* drunk. I'm sorry, Ma. The truth is I just wanted one night alone at a hotel with my girlfriend. If that's so terrible, well then, I'm a terrible man." I go over to rub Maddie's back, and by uttering two sentences, I'm the favorite guy of all four females in this room, at least for the moment.

And then my dad hustles off to the kitchen because Nonna is yelling for him, Casey's husband calls out for her and Penelope to come watch his favorite scene in *Christmas with the Kranks*, and my ma hollers, "Eddie. Eddie! *Edward Sullivan Cannavale!* Declan's here with his girlfriend! Get out here, come on!" She shakes her head at us. "That boy's been in the guest room the whole time since he got here except when we're eatin'."

I shake my head, rolling my eyes, grateful that my little brother is being a slightly bigger disappointment than I am once again.

My ma disappears to get the platter just as my little brother emerges from the hallway, sliding his phone into the front pocket of his sweatpants. He's so fucking handsome I want to punch him in the face, but I also want to pick him up and cradle him in my arms because he's my baby brother.

"Eddie. You little shit. This is my girlfriend, Maddie."

His face lights up. "Oh, hey. How you doin'?" my brother says, grinning and doing a Joey from *Friends* imitation because he's a sweet, dumbass flirt. He takes Maddie's hand to shake it and doesn't let go.

"Well hello there. Wow. Declan wasn't kidding when he said you were ugly," she deadpans.

"Poor guy. I hear he was the best-looking in the family until I was born."

She narrows her eyes at him, and I want to throw a blanket over his head already. "I think I've seen you on my niece's wall…"

Shit. She recognizes him.

He smirks. "Tell your niece I said 'hey.'"

"She's thirteen," I tell him as I pull his hand from hers. "Idiot."

"Tell her I say 'hey' in five years," he clarifies. My twenty-six-year-old brother has been playing a high school student in various pieces of crap for the past eight years, but he's currently the star of a very popular show, and I'm really proud of him, even though he's totally wasting his life in Los Angeles like an idiot. Or in Vancouver, Canada, really, because that's where all of those shows are shot.

Maddie asks me to take a picture of them—to send to her niece—and I do it because I'm an awesome fake boyfriend who isn't at all jealous of the fact that she hasn't asked for a picture of *me* to send to Piper. Then, when I hand her phone back to her, she holds it out to Eddie and asks him to take a picture of us so she can send it to Piper. She wraps her arms around my waist, and I put mine around her shoulders, and I don't ever want to let go.

My ma comes out of the kitchen with two cans of

Guinness for me and Eddie. "Drink fast, and don't let your nonna see you with this."

I raise my Guinness to Eddie and try my brogue on Maddie again. "May the hinges of our friendship never grow rusty." I glance over and catch Maddie's eyelashes flutter.

Because Eddie's a hot shot actor, he raises his pint of the black stuff to Maddie and Ma and says in his comparatively mediocre brogue, "May you have all the happiness and luck that life can hold, and at the end of your rainbows, may you find a pot of gold."

Fuck you, Eddie.

"Deadly," Maddie sighs, fanning herself. But she's just being polite to my brother.

My ma winks at me. Then she takes Maddie by the arm. "Come, my dear. It's time to feed you to the Italian wolf. You want a pop?"

Maddie glances back at me, confused.

"A soda," I translate for her.

"Oh. Sure. Thanks, Mamie. Whatever you're having."

"Well, I've been sipping Jameson from a flask, but I can mix it with a Coke if you want an Irish cola."

"That sounds perfect." They wink at each other conspiratorially.

My brother and I both watch Maddie go.

Eddie swallows a big gulp of stout, sighs loudly, and proclaims, "She's hot."

I smack the back of his head while still guzzling my contraband Irish beer.

"What? She is."

"I know that. So where's *your* girlfriend?"

"She's in LA, actually. With her family."

"Oh yeah? Is it that friend of yours? From college?"

"Who—Birdie?" He forces a laugh. "Nerdy Birdie? No. She only dates other nerds. She's a nerd snob. And so not my type."

"You sure about that? Because your voice always changes when you talk about her."

"You know what—remind me never to hire you as my lawyer because you're not as good at reading people as you think you are. My new *girlfriend's* name is Alana. She lives in New York." He grins. "She's a model. So hot."

I roll my eyes. "That sounds promising."

"She's not like the other ones—this one's really cool. I mean, not cool but smart. Not smart like Birdie, but she's not dumb."

"Uh-huh. You bringing her to the wedding?"

"Nah. She goes to the Bahamas every year for New Year's with her friends. We're both just busy with work."

"Right. She lives in New York. And you live in LA and you're always working in Vancouver."

He lowers his voice and turns his back to the kitchen so the rest of our family can't hear him. "I haven't actually met her in person yet."

"I knew it."

"She slid into my DMs on Instagram, and we've been texting and FaceTiming." He waggles his eyebrows, so I know he means he's seen her naked. "For over a month now."

"You've had FaceTime sex, is what you're saying?"

"Nope. I mean, she's sent me pictures of her naked, of course."

"Of course."

"But she doesn't want to do any sex stuff until we actually meet. She's old-fashioned that way. It's sweet. Not sweet like Birdie, but she's polite. Different. Not quirky like Birdie. But I like her."

I pat him on the shoulder. "That's adorable."

"Welp. As always, I aspire to be like you, bro. I'll get me a good woman, and then hopefully I can play a lawyer on TV one day and get paid even more than you do."

He's not kidding. He has always wanted to be like me, get himself a good woman, and play a lawyer or a doctor on TV. Why he keeps dating models and starlets, I'll never understand. But everything feels right in the world with about nine ounces of Guinness entering my bloodstream, a nice fire burning in the fireplace, and my current favorite brother by my side.

And then I'm reminded of what a cold, shitty world it had been for me for most of the year when the front door opens, and my former closest brother and the woman I once thought I'd marry walk through it.

TWENTY-TWO

Maddie

I *WISH* GRANDMA GOT RUN OVER BY A REINDEER

So. Much. Seafood. It smells like an Italian aquarium in the Cannavale kitchen, and Declan was not kidding about his nonna not liking me.

Mamie is surreptitiously pouring whiskey into a glass of Coke behind the matriarch's back, and Nonna is eyeing me suspiciously after being told that I'm Declan's new girlfriend.

"Oh yeah?" is all she says, frowning. She looks like a miniature Robert De Niro in drag—but kinda pretty! I guess the festive Christmas apron that says ***Baking Spirits Bright*** is being worn ironically. "*Hmph.*" She goes back to stirring a cauldron of fish broth.

"It's very nice to meet you..."

"Francesca," Mamie tells me since Nonna does not offer her name.

"Francesca. That's a beautiful name. Declan's told me so much about you."

She glances back at me while adding fresh basil, salt, and pepper to the broth. "This is what you are wearing to my dinner?" She shakes her head, frowning even more intensely. "Not smart. Or maybe you *don'* wanna eat my food?"

Everyone else is wearing either sweats or oversized trousers, and yeah, I should have listened to my hot fake boyfriend. "Oh, I very much plan to eat your food, Mrs. Cannavale. Declan did tell me to change what I was wearing, but I..." No use finishing that sentence since she isn't paying any attention to me. She's too busy pouring mussels and clams into the fish broth.

Mamie comes over to hand me the Jameson and Coke, which I gulp down immediately. God bless her, she was not stingy with the whiskey. She takes the gift bag from me and holds it up to show Nonna. "Look what Maddie brought you. A gift from her hotel!"

"Open for me," she mumbles as she pours oil into a huge saucepan.

Mamie pulls out the shot glass with the Cleveland skyline etched onto it. "Cute, right? It's Cleveland. Your favorite city after Sicily."

Nonna eyes it warily. "*Hmph.*" She flicks her hand in the air. "Put away somewhere. I got no time for it."

Mamie turns and rolls her eyes at me, grinning impishly. "She means thank you for being sooooo thoughtful." She pops the shot glass back into the bag and places it on a chair by the kitchen table because every inch of the counters and tables in here are covered with ingredients and plates and platters and baskets of food.

Guess I should just start listening to Declan. He was right about the pants, and he was right about his parents and nonna not caring if I bring them gifts or not. But I had to do something. Especially if some woman who's dated *two* Cannavale sons is going to be here tonight.

He said he met her in college, and they were on and off for a decade. *A decade.* I wonder if he had sex with her in this house. I wonder how much he still thinks about her. All this time I've known him, he's probably been in a bad mood because he was upset about her. I hate that I didn't know that. Or maybe I hate *her* for doing this to him. Out of loyalty. Because I'm his assistant. And it's my job to be loyal to him.

Welp. So much for resisting my boss! As if seeing him dance around naked to a seventies pop song wasn't enough—watching him with his niece made my ovaries throb, and I don't know if my "No Sleepovers" rule is going to prevent the rest of me from falling for him. Hopefully he'll go back to being an insufferable ass when we get back to work. Hopefully I'm only staring at the kitchen table, picturing him eating breakfast in here as a teenager and wondering what kind of cereal he ate because I'm bored. Or maybe he wasn't as good at sex as I thought he was last night. Maybe I was mistaken. Maybe he's not as sweet or caring as he seems to be lately. It could all be an act.

Or maybe I'm screwed.

But at least I'm being screwed by a real man for a change. Screwed long and hard and every which way but upside-down. Actually, we may have done an upside-down thing last night too. "Can I help with anything?" I blurt out before I start moaning Declan's name in front of his mother and grandmother.

They're in the middle of arguing about how much marinara sauce they'll need, so my question goes ignored. But when Declan walks in, they both shut up and start grinning. Even his own flesh and blood are not immune to his handsome face.

I can tell immediately that his mood has changed, though.

"*Ciao, bella,*" he says to his nonna, kissing her on the cheek. "When do we eat? I'm starving. Why do my pants still fit me, huh? What a rip-off."

"*Ciao, bello,*" she mumbles. "It's time," she announces, still scooping deep-fried calamari into a bowl. "Time for antipasti. Get back out there, uh! *Andiamo andiamo*!"

It's not even four o'clock yet, but I guess it'll take about three hours to eat all of this food.

Declan puts his arm around my shoulders without looking at me. "Hey."

"Hey."

"You ready?" Something tells me he isn't asking me if I'm ready for dinner.

"As I'll ever be."

He pushes the swinging door open, and I walk out to the dining area. There are a bunch of people in the living room all of a sudden, but Declan goes straight to the table and takes a seat with his back to the living room. Hunched over, like a moody teenager. Like the Little Bummer Boy. With Dean Martin singing "Rudolph the Red Nosed Reindeer" and all the decorations around him, his gloominess is almost comical. He gestures for me to sit next to him, but when I notice the couple in the corner who are staring at me, I can't move. That must be Brady and Hannah.

Hannah is a petite blonde who somehow looks stunning, elegant, and adorable in an oversized blouse and overalls with a Santa Mickey appliqued on the front pocket. I don't know what I was expecting—a Disney witch or a Sophia Loren type —but I wasn't expecting a midwestern Tinkerbell. She's all glow-y and smiley. She's the opposite of me, and I want to hate her, but I can't. I can't even hate Brady, who's a lankier, artsier version of Declan. They're both touching each other in that gentle, instinctive way that couples do when they're in love.

I'm starving too, all of a sudden, and it's not for antipasti.

It's Eddie who finally introduces me to the people I haven't met yet. Aiden must be the oldest—handsome and starting to go a little gray around the sideburns. He has a wife and two kids. Casey's husband looks like a TV high school football coach. This family may be a little loud, but they look like the stock photo of a family that comes with a picture frame. When Eddie introduces me to Brady and Hannah, they look a little tense. Like they're expecting me to tear them a new one or something.

"Merry Christmas" is all I say. "Congratulations."

Hannah seems relieved, but Brady says, "Thank you. I'd congratulate you too, but you snagged yourself the worst brother."

Hannah smacks him, somewhat playfully.

"Hey, I'll take what I can get."

"It's really nice to meet you," Hannah says, giving my arm a friendly little squeeze.

"All right! Everyone sit down!" Tony orders as Nonna carries a tureen out to the table. "This is not a drill! Kids—you're eating in the family room. Stay out of trouble."

"Come and get your dinner, *love*," I sing into Declan's ear as I take the seat beside him.

"Smartass," he whispers into mine. He's not happy, but at least he doesn't look miserable anymore.

Casey makes a joke about Hannah's wedding dress, and Hannah tells her she scheduled the final fitting for after Christmas for a reason. And then everyone looks at Declan, who's frowning at the empty plate in front of him, and it's really, really awkward. I want to give him a verbal spanking, but I also want to give him a hug. And I also want him to give me an actual spanking later, maybe.

Tony Cannavale rushes through grace. "Bless us, O Lord, and these, Thy gifts, which we are about to receive Thy bounty, through Christ, our Lord, Amen." He barely waits for everyone else to say "Amen" before continuing, "And I just wanna say…"

He smacks one hand down on the table, shaking the whole thing. "I'm just gonna say this once... This tension here, between certain someones, and the taking sides and the bickering and the angry awkward silence and the what have you. I will have none of it. Not tonight. No more. We're all family here. All right? All of us. We celebrate love in this house. For everyone. That's all I'm saying about it—everybody eat."

"*Mangia, mangia,*" Nonna grumbles.

I place my hand on Declan's thigh under the table, and his hand is immediately covering mine. He doesn't look at anyone, but he's touching me, and that's enough.

Tony explains the menu to me, since I'm the only one who's never been to Christmas Eve dinner here before. "Traditionally, Italians don't eat meat on Christmas Eve, which is why all the fish—seven kinds of fish. But my mama makes her own rules, and she also makes three different kinds of meatballs in honor of my pops, who loved meatballs." Tony and Nonna cross themselves without pausing their eating. "The meatballs are *secondi*. So leave room for them."

"Hey, do we know how you and asshat met?" Casey asks me.

I swallow a calamari and then tell her, "Asshat convention." Declan rubs my thigh, reminding me that it's okay to tell them that I work for him. "Actually, we met at work. We started working together two months ago."

"Oh, are you a real estate agent?"

"She's my executive assistant," Declan says, slurping his clam and mussel *posillopo*. He turns to me and says, "Best I've ever had. On every level. Don't know what I'd do without her."

"Nonna, can I have the recipe for this soup? Whatever you put in it, I need to feed it to him every day."

"No," she snarls.

"It's not the soup, it's the Guinness," Mamie stage whispers. "Every nice word out of that boy's mouth is from the Irish side. Everything good my boys got to give a woman is from the Irish side."

I share a look and a sly grin with Hannah and Aiden's wife.

I don't know about that, Mrs. C, but what your boy's got is awfully good.

TWENTY-THREE

Declan

IT'S BEGINNING TO LOOK A LOT LIKE UNFINISHED BUSINESS

While everyone else is crowding into the family room to play Christmas Carol Pictionary with the kids, I pull Maddie into the guest bathroom with me and shut the door. I had wine with dinner. I'm feeling really full and warm. And I caught her unbuttoning and unzipping her jeans about an hour ago, and I just can't wait to get my hands on that warm, round belly.

"Declan," she whispers. "What are you doing?"

I lift her sweater up, drop to my knees, and kiss the flesh that's bulging out of her tight jeans.

"Are you out of your mind?"

"Yes, and I need to get you out of these pants."

"Seriously? You're horny right now? I can't even think about sex—I can barely even breathe."

I try to get her pants down, but they won't budge, not even an inch.

"Declan." She puts her hands on either side of my face and pulls me up. I fucking love it when she puts her hands on my face. I try to kiss her mouth, but she dodges out of the way.

"Hey. What's wrong?"

She frowns at me. "What's wrong is you need to talk to Hannah, and you need to talk to Brady. I don't care if you talk to them separately or together, but you need to talk to them."

I shrug. "About what?"

"Dec."

"Hey, you've never called me Dec before. I like it."

"*Mr. Cannavale.* You need to talk to your ex and your brother. In private. I'm telling you this as your assistant whose job it is to make you a less terrible person."

"I don't recall giving you those instructions when I hired you."

"It's something I do pro bono."

"Then we're on the same page. I am very *pro bono* right now too. Take those pants off." I make one last attempt at getting her pants down, but they're attached to her. They're mean, and I hate them.

"Declan. I mean it."

"So do I. Take off your pants." I finally look up at her beautiful sexy face, and her eyes are glistening. With tears. I don't think I've ever seen her look so serious. "Baby…"

"Dec. If you can't talk to them, at least let them talk to you. Please. For me."

For her.

Shit.

"Will you?"

"Yes."

"Tonight?"

"Yes. Right now. I will do that. For you…my long-suffering assistant."

She nods. "And newly suffering fake girlfriend."

"Right." I stare down at her mouth, her quivering lower lip.

"Declan."

"Right. So that's a *no* re. the quickie?"

"It's a *no* re. me ever getting these jeans off again, I think."

I stare down at those curves. "I can focus on the top front quadrant and get you out of here in three minutes."

She tries to laugh and gives me a playful shove. "Ooof. I need to lie down. Go deal with your emotional baggage." She slips away from me, opening the door.

"You coming too?"

She presses her back against the wall, trying to breathe. "Just leave me here. Save yourself!"

I manage to steal two kisses before going to deal with my emotional baggage. Because kissing my assistant and my fake girlfriend is more fun than dealing with my ex and my former best friend.

I stand in the doorway to the family room and wait for Hannah and Brady to notice me. Everyone's still writing things down on scraps of paper. Hannah and Brady are on the same team, of course. I guess they always have been. Not that they were cheating when Hannah and I were together. I believed my brother when he told me that. But they look like they've been a couple forever.

I couldn't bring myself to look at pictures of Hannah and me for months after I got the news. But I looked through old photos of us about a month ago. We were a good-looking pair of people, that's for certain. And I did love her. And I know she loved me. But I look at them, and I think about what we looked like together, and it wasn't what I'm seeing before me now. We were two people who loved each other and were trying to make a relationship work. Hannah and Brady are a couple. Simple as that.

I finally catch Brady's eye when he drops a few pieces of paper into the bowl. I point back and forth between him and Hannah and then to myself and then gesture down the hall. He gives me an incredulous look and mouths *Dude*.

I roll my eyes and then mouth to him, *Not a three-way. Idiot. Talking.* I make the international sign of talking with my hand.

He looks so damn happy I could cry. He gives his fiancée a little nudge and nods in my direction, whispering in her ear. She nods, tells Casey to start without them. I go to the living room to take a seat in the armchair. The power seat. I sit like Al Pacino in *The Godfather II*.

And then I hear Maddie's voice in my head,

reminding me that this isn't a negotiation, and I reassemble myself in a more friendly pose.

They walk in together, side-by-side but not hand-in-hand, which was thoughtful of them. They take a seat on the loveseat near me but don't sit too close together. As if that makes them any less engaged. They don't have to bother trying to make things easier for me now.

Everything hurts a little less since last night.

Everything except the thought of what will happen when the holidays are over.

"Hi, Dec." Hannah is the first to speak. Hannah was always the first to speak. I could always rely on her to keep the wheels spinning, even when I was so busy working that I forgot we had wheels. "Thanks for finally talking to us."

"I know you both tried to get in touch with me… I *was* busy."

"I understand why you didn't want to hear from me. I won't speak for Brady."

"You can speak for me, babe," Brady says. And he isn't even being sarcastic. "You'll probably swear less, so that's good." He doesn't grin or smirk.

Hannah proceeds to say every single thing that she already said half a year ago, in voice mail messages and emails that I didn't respond to. She tells me what she wants me to hear. I let her talk because it makes her feel better. It's what I always did, back when we were together. I thought it was enough.

Brady's four years older than me. When I first found out they'd gotten engaged, I felt betrayed, sure.

But I also couldn't believe Hannah would want to marry a guy who teaches anthropology at a liberal arts college in Ohio instead of a corporate lawyer in Manhattan. It didn't make sense. Unless I was a total failure of a human being who didn't deserve love from Hannah or anyone else.

I figured Brady's everything I'm not. I figured I was the put-upon hero in this story. The guy who was trying to become someone better for the girl. And then I wasn't given the chance to make things right, and that's what sucked. But I was in another story all along. He's everything she needs. Hannah deserves everything she wants. I know now that I was saving my everything for someone else. I just needed to meet that person. And now I need to figure out how to give it to her.

Hannah finally stops talking and waits for my response.

"I understand," I say. "I'm happy for you guys. Really, I am."

"I mean, I'm sorry it hurt you," Brady says, staring down at my feet. "But I'm also not sorry." He finally takes Hannah's hand. "Because I always loved her. She belongs with me."

"Yeah. I know."

"Then why the fuck have you been such a dick all this time?"

Hannah squeezes my brother's thigh. "I think a better question would be—why is he less of a dick now?" she says with a knowing look.

"Why, indeed," I muse.

"I'll let you guys talk some more. Catch up." Hannah gives my brother a kiss on the cheek and musses my hair as she passes by, leaving us alone together.

It's been so long since I've talked to Brady.

We watch Hannah go and then stare at the twinkling lights on the fake tree and listen to Dean Martin sing "Silver Bells" for the twentieth time tonight, and every single time you hear it you just have to wonder if it's playing at the right speed… And then he stands up first, and I pop up, and we're hugging for the first time all year, *and fuck you family holidays and long overdue reconciliation*, you're not gonna make me cry.

We let go of each other at the same time, shoving each other away because we aren't giant pussies. We sit back down, and when I see him touching the corner of his eye with his finger, I do the same. Because I'm so sad for him for being such a fucking cornball.

"I wanted to make you Best Man," he tells me in a hushed voice. "Asshole."

"Well, that makes sense," I say. "I am the best."

He shakes his head at me.

"And also the worst. I know. I am sorry. I'll still be in the wedding party though."

"Yeah. But you were always my best friend. I mean, except for those four years when you weren't born yet. And for the past half a year that you were being a total dick." He reaches over to punch my arm.

"Right back at you. Fuckhead." I squeeze his face with one hand.

He pushes me away. "Whatever. Aiden's all excited about planning the bachelor party. You better come to that now."

I wrinkle my nose. "Aiden's planning it? In Cleveland?"

"It's gonna suck so hard. You have to come. Come oooooon." He affects a Boston accent. "The wicked pissah Boston cousins are gonna be there. It'll be bomb! It'll be sick!" He shrugs his shoulders. "I don't think the Italians are gonna make it." His eyes fill with mock terror as he puts his hand on my shoulder and squeezes. "But the Irish, Dec. Save me from the Irish."

I'm shaking my head because that is a hard *no*. When we went drinking with the Bostons and the Irish back when Aiden got married, I lost track of two entire days and woke up in Michigan.

"*Ach*. It's been donkey's years since we were on the tear with them *morans*. But noooooo. Feck off."

"You have to. Least you could do."

"Right. Least I could do for providing you with your bride." God, there's nothing better than being able to joke about something that once felt like the end of the world.

"Tell you what. You come to my bachelor party—I'll be your best man when you marry Maddie." He gives me a wink. "I can tell Nonna approves."

"Yeah. She's ignoring her instead of picking on her."

"Good sign."

"Great sign."

"It seems like it's…still new."

I'm dying to tell him everything. He's a fucking anthropologist—if anyone can help me understand why I felt the need to ask my assistant to pretend to be my girlfriend instead of just asking her out, it's him. He could put some kind of cultural perspective on this. But I already know what's up. I didn't want her to think it's real, because I thought it would be easier if she wants everything to go back to the way things used to be, in January. I thought *I* might want everything to go back to the way things used to be.

Except I barely even remember how things used to be before I could call her baby without her rolling her eyes at me. Before I knew what it felt like to hear her say my name when she was coming. Before I knew just how hard it would be to pretend that I don't ever want to go back to the way things used to be.

"Yeah. It's still new" is what I say. "She's great. Really great. But we'll see how it goes." What I really mean is, we'll just have to wait and see how I screw this one up. And I'm wondering if it's better for both of us if I just screw it all up now instead of later.

But then I see Maddie come down the stairs with Ma. She's wearing a pair of my ma's cranberry-colored velour track pants. And, impossibly, I'm still attracted to her. I still have this insane urge to put a zeppola in her oven. And nothing has ever felt so right.

Speaking of zeppole, Nonna wheels out the dessert cart. It's piled high with Italian donuts, struffoli, panettone, cannoli, tiramisu, and the best coffee in Ohio. About forty million calories and as many reasons why Maddie and I probably won't be getting it on tonight. But nothing will stop me from trying.

TWENTY-FOUR

Maddie

WINTER BLUNDERLAND

I guess I shouldn't have had those two glasses of wine after the Irish cola. I definitely should not have eaten those last three zeppole. Or the giant slice of panettone. Or the struffoli or the cannoli or the tiramisu. And for that matter, I probably should have also passed on the spaghetti with anchovies and the deep-fried cod. And the meatballs. But it was all so fucking delicious, and I was afraid Nonna would stab me with a fork if I didn't try all of her food.

So, I don't really regret eating any of it.

I just wish I could have somehow digested it all within an hour so I could fully appreciate the fact that a seriously gorgeous man has his hand up my sweater and is kissing my neck as we ride the elevator up to his hotel room. Or my hotel room. Or just any place with a floor that I can lie down on for a while. And maybe take a half-hour nap.

I'm twenty-eight years old and my jeans are rolled up in my purse, and I'm wearing a sixty-year-old lady's cranberry-red velour track pants. I need to take a nap and maybe make myself throw up a little so I can have a lot of hot sex with my hot sexy boss who is also my very temporary fake boyfriend. I am winning at life.

"I've been thinking about these tits all night," he mumbles.

My back is flat against one side of the elevator and my arms are just hanging lifelessly, even though I really want to run my fingers through Declan's hair and squeeze his butt, and I want to rip his clothes off and lick his abs and kiss him all over, except I can't lift my hands.

"Mmph" is all I'm able to respond with, and I think that sums it all up.

"This elevator moves too fast," he grumbles.

"Ugh. Yeah."

"I'm going to do bad, bad, dirty bad things to you when we get to my room."

"Mmkay."

"What're you gonna do to me?"

"Mmm. Gonna lie down on you."

"Yeah?"

"And not move for a while."

"Mmmmm."

"And close my eyes."

"Yessss."

The elevator comes to an earth-shattering, shitty,

terrible, mean abrupt stop, and then the doors ding and slide open.

Declan and I just stare out at the hallway and continue to use the wall and each other to prop ourselves up.

"Shit," I whisper. "We have to move so we don't go back down again."

"I'm gonna go back down on *you*—"

"Okay, seriously, we have to move." I manage to slide sideways and stop the doors from closing with my foot, and Declan's forehead slams against the wall.

"Fuck."

"Shit! Sorry!"

"I'm fine." He groans. "Nooooo pain."

He puts his hand out to hold the doors open so I can slip into the hallway. I don't remember elevators being this difficult to use, but they're really very dangerous and complicated. I pull him out into the hallway with me so the doors don't close on him, and I guess the adrenaline rush of nearly dying is giving me strength, because I yank him so hard that he stumbles and takes me with him, and we fall to the carpet in slow motion.

Fortunately, our bones are rubbery, and we have a few extra inches of carb padding to cushion the fall.

So now this is happening.

I'm on my back on the floor—which is all I ever wanted—and Declan is facedown, and we're both laughing so hard we can't breathe.

I mean, we could barely breathe before because of the carb padding.

"Are you okay?" I finally manage to ask.

"I totally meant to do that." He hikes himself up onto his elbows, and I swear to God, he still looks sexy right now. "Should we just fuck right here, maybe?"

"Sure."

"Cool."

We both stay exactly where we are for thirty seconds or maybe an hour, and then we slowly crawl toward his room, which is closer, and lean against the door.

"I'm going to stand up now," he declares.

"I'm going to watch you do that."

He slides up the door, going up, up, up.

"I'm so proud of you!"

"I'm just getting started making you proud, baby," he says as he fumbles around, trying to find the key card in his pocket.

The seventh or eighth time he slides the key card through, I hear a little beep, and then the door that I'm sitting and leaning against opens, and now I'm lying on the floor again.

Which is great.

"Oops," he says about ten seconds after it happened, because he's unbuckled his belt and let his pants drop to the floor and I'm so fucking jealous. "I got you. Hang on." He bends down, grabs my wrists, and pulls me across the carpet until my feet clear the door and it closes.

"Thanks."

"I saved you." He lies down alongside me, with his

head by my feet. "I need to get you out of my ma's pants."

"Okay."

He tugs at one of the pant legs for a while. "I can't."

"That's okay." I close my eyes and rub my belly. "Merry Christmas."

"Merry Christmas, baby." I feel his head on my breast. Not kissing it or anything. He's just laying his head upon it. "We're gonna lie here like this for ten minutes, and then I will fuck you like an animal."

"You got it, champ."

I'm not exactly sure how it works, anatomically, but I am one hundred percent certain that there is no room left in me for his penis. Not even the tip. And I am ten thousand percent sure that my body is too busy digesting to let me have even the tiniest orgasm.

Which really sucks.

Because I want his penis in me.

And I would love to have an orgasm.

I want as many orgasms and as much of his penis as I can get before we have to go back to the way things were.

But I also really like lying here and not moving.

He taps one finger against my thigh. "Question." His voice is muffled because my boob is in his face. "When do we have to get up in the morning?"

"Oh. Right. Six o'clock."

"Fuck that."

"We have to. Limo's picking us up at seven thirty.

Unless you want to take a later…um…what do you call it? Flight."

"No, I want to ride to the place with you. The airport."

"Good. I tried to get us on the same flight this morning, but I couldn't do it."

"You did?"

"Uh-huh. But I did change my tickets so we can fly together for the wedding stuff."

"You did?!"

"Yup. And I got us one room at the Ritz-Carlton. A suite."

"I love that." He strokes my hair like I'm an adorable, obedient puppy. "That's good. You're good. I want that."

"Good." I somehow manage to wrap my arms around his neck, but it takes a really long time and a lot of effort. "Dec?"

"Yeah."

"Can we just get in bed and put on a movie and not move at all?"

"I thought you'd never ask." He moves his head a little to kiss my boob, somewhere around my armpit area. "You're amazing. I'm gonna help you up."

"Thanks."

He slowly sits up and slowly, very slowly, stands up with the help of the wall beside him. And then he helps me up and we take a few wobbly steps and then collapse onto the bed together. "I'm taking your shirt off though," he says.

"I'm taking yours off too then," I insist.

We take each other's shirts off at the same time, and I wish someone were filming this so I can watch it later because I have no idea how we're able to do this. We crawl up to the pillows, he finds the TV remote on the bedside table, and he turns on *Gremlins*. We both say, "I love this movie" at the same time and then turn to kiss each other and bump noses.

"Ow." I rub my nose.

"Shit." He rubs my nose. "We suck."

"I'm actually really turned on by you right now."

"Really?" His face lights up, and he places his hand on my hip.

"Yes, but if you touch any of my lady bits tonight, it will probably kill me."

He rolls onto his back, groaning. "*Mannaggia*, Nonna! You cockblocker!" He shakes his fist in the air and then takes in a slow, shaky breath. "Yeah, it would kill me too. Rain check?"

"Rain *checks*."

He holds his hand up for me to slap him five, and I do, gently. After a while, I say, "I had a really good time tonight though. I'm glad you made up with Brady and Hannah. Are you?"

"Yeah. Definitely. Thanks for making me slightly less terrible."

"Always a pleasure." I give him a nudge and ask him something that I've been dying to ask him for days. "Tell me about the tattoo on your arm," I whisper. "It's a swallow?"

"Yeah."

"When'd you get it?"

"College. It was Hannah's idea." He moves his arm so I can see the flying bird on the inside of his bicep. "She got one on the back of her neck. So when I put my arm around her shoulder, they were touching. They'd match up."

"That's sweet."

"Yeah. She said that swallows are a symbol of everlasting love and loyalty. Because swallows mate for life."

I trace the edge of the tattoo with my fingertip. His muscles instinctively flex, and it's adorable. I kiss the bird's face. I use all my energy to move my body over enough to kiss Declan's beautiful sad face.

"I'm sorry you were hurt by them."

He shrugs. "I guess people can't really help who they fall in love with…"

"No. I guess not."

"To be honest, in some ways, I envy them for just doing what they want. Without thinking about the consequences."

"Well, yeah. If it weren't for people like them, all lawyers would be out of a job."

I don't hear him laughing, so I turn my head and instantly regret making a joke.

"Anyway," he says without looking at me. "I went to get the tattoo removed, earlier this year. But the guy said it was a really good one and that he sometimes does swallows for people who think of them—all birds—as a symbol of freedom. So, I kept it."

"Do you like being free?"

"I like being free for the right woman… I really

like being free to pretend to be the right woman's boyfriend."

Oh, the words. Sometimes his words penetrate me like a big hard cock, and sometimes they kiss me gently on the lips. I kiss his tattoo again and roll onto my back, staring up at the ceiling.

"Cooper..." he whispers. It sounds like his eyes are closed.

"Yeah?"

"Don't go back to your room tonight."

"I have to."

"No you don't."

"Fine. But only because I can't move. Just promise me you won't say anything else that will make me like you."

"You know I can't promise that. Everything I say makes you like me, Coop."

Mannaggia, Declan Cannavale. I don't know for sure what *mannaggia* means, but he's right.

"I can't move my eyes, but imagine me rolling my eyes right now."

"I can't move my head, but imagine me kissing you right now."

Mannaggia.

TWENTY-FIVE

Declan

I'D HAVE A BLUE BALLS CHRISTMAS WITHOUT YOU

I remember when I was eight, waking up on Christmas morning to find that it had snowed overnight. I finally got the bike that I'd been begging for all year. Nonna was in Italy, so Ma made waffles with ice cream for breakfast. We watched TV and drank hot chocolate all day. That was a great Christmas.

But it was a load of horse shit compared to this one because Maddie Cooper's hands and mouth are all over me. She's pressing her body against my back and she feels naked, and her soft gasps and moans are the only alarm clock I ever want to wake up to. Both Maddie and my cock woke up before me, and I'm glad I had time to digest last night's dinner because all the blood in my body has headed south, and it just might stay there for the rest of the winter.

I open my eyes to find that the room is still dark. The clock on the bedside table says it's 5:25, and she said we have to get up at six, so we have time for this. I have all the time in the world for this. She's exploring my body and I don't want to disturb her because everything she's doing, as always, is so very right. She is definitely making me feel like a less terrible person. A very hard, not very terrible, really fucking horny person. But I'll just lie here on my side and let her do her thing for as long as possible.

She kisses my back, her lips and tongue making her way down that side of me while her smooth, determined hands travel across and up and down my chest and abs. Curious about my chest hair, investigating the dips and contours of every muscle. She can probably tell that I'm awake because my breaths are coming harder and faster, chest rising and falling beneath her fingers, abs tightening under her palms. She may never be able to read my mind the way I want her to, but if she wants to read my body, then I am an open book.

One leg bends, slinking around and encircling mine as she undulates behind me.

She grazes one hand up my arm, barely touching me, and it makes me shudder all over.

No woman has ever made me shudder like that before.

The electricity that has always crackled between us is still there, but the tension has transformed into pure, uninhibited want. It's easily enough energy to fuel a lifetime of lust between us. I used to wonder if

I'd be happy enough with just Hannah for the rest of my days, but the only question I have when it comes to Maddie is—is it too soon for me to retire? Because I don't know how I'll ever be able to get through an entire workday if I know I could be having sex with her instead.

I stroke her smooth leg, the one that's wrapped around mine.

She removes the one arm from under me, sits up, her nipples skimming across the skin of my back as she does, and as if that weren't enough, she kisses my shoulder, palming my excruciating erection through my boxer briefs.

"Babyyyy," I whisper.

"Shhhh" is all she says. And then her leg slips from beneath my hand, her hand slips inside my boxer briefs as she slides them down to my ankles, and I feel her mouth and teeth on the flesh of my butt and *holy shit I like it.* She nudges me onto my back. I kick my underwear off and grab on to her hips when she straddles my waist, the cool air rushing in when she sits up and the covers slide down her torso. But it's the silhouette of her naked body that causes me to shiver.

It's the way she licks my pec and twirls her tongue around the nipple, and then, sweet Jesus, she licks me all the way from my pelvis up to my chin and then kisses me with such passion. The way she sucks on my tongue, the little sing-song animal sounds she makes when she nibbles on my lower lip and places quick, playful pecks all over my face. I'm melting into her and into the mattress at the same time. I've never been too big on kissing, but I could kiss this woman forever, I think. Just when I've committed myself to doing that, she pulls away, slides farther down, giving me a hint of what her wet pussy would feel like on my cock.

I groan, and I cross my arms tight over my face. Because if I look and see her head bobbing up and down, I will explode in her gorgeous mouth. If I see her look up at me down there, eyelids heavy, licking her lips and grinning, I will ask her to marry me, and if she says no my life would be over. She kisses up the inside of my thigh, teasing me, driving me crazy. I'd expect nothing less from a succubus. The tip of her tongue trails up the underside of my shaft and then swirls around the head, flicking just beneath it and then sucking and *fuck.* I reach down to grab fistfuls of her silky hair because I need to touch her.

One of her hands is gripping my ass, the other follows her warm mouth up and down, up and down. Determined and confident but gentle, that's how she's always handled me. She has been the boss of me, and if she didn't know it before, she must know it now.

I tug on her hair, whisper her name through clenched teeth, and she knows it's time to stop if she wants to keep this going any longer.

Her body is pressed against mine again, she whispers in my ear, I hear the words "pill," I hear the word "clean," I'm nodding and saying "yes, fuck yes." Because *yes. Fuck yes.* This woman is just full of great ideas, and I like her so much.

She places one hand flat on my chest for leverage

and wraps the other around my rock-hard cock, lowering herself carefully and slowly. We're both holding our breaths, because that's what you do when you know your life is about to change. That's not an exaggeration. I mean, I really wanted that bike when I was eight, but I have never wanted anything more than I've wanted to come inside Maddie Cooper.

When she's finally lowered herself down onto me and wriggled around a tiny bit to make herself comfortable, and drive me just a little bit crazier, we both exhale. She leans back, resting her hands on my thighs, tits swollen and silently begging for me. She rocks her hips, nice and slow. I reach up to cup her breasts, because no man on earth could resist them, but I'm the only one who gets to touch them now.

Finally, because I'm still me, I break the silence with: "I thought we said no Christmas presents."

"Shhh. Don't talk. Just let me do this."

"Not even dirty talk?"

She thinks about it for a hot second and then shakes her head and covers my mouth with her hand.

"Roger that," I mumble. She doesn't want me to talk right now because everything I say makes her like me more. So I will save the dirty talk for later. For now, I let her do this. I let her do that. I'll let her do whatever she wants. There are a million things I want to say to her, but I have to tell her this one thing right now. "You are so fucking beautiful, Maddie." I wrap one hand around the back of her neck and pull her down for a kiss. Hard and fast, and then I let her go.

It sets her on fire, and she bears down on me. Nice

and slow becomes swift and feverish. Back and forth, round and round, up and down. She's unhinged, stunning, and I wish there were more light so I could really see her right now because I bet she's radiant.

God, I want to come, but I would rather die than come before she does.

So I'm mentally reciting the employee dating policy in the Sentinel human resources handbook and wondering if I'm too big of an ass to be able to maintain a good relationship with my assistant while we're working together. I know the answer, and I don't like it. But it just makes me want to give her all I've got to give right now.

Shhh. Don't talk, Maddie reminds me in my head. *Just let me do this.* If that's all I ever have to do—keep my mouth shut and let her do whatever she needs to do—then I might actually be able to make this work.

She slows and sways, and I force my eyes open so I can watch in awe as the waves of orgasm take over her body. My name escapes her lips, mingles with some *fucks*, a few *Oh Gods,* and when she reaches a crescendo, that's when it's time for *me* to take over her body.

I get her on her back, lift one leg to rest it on my shoulder, and drive into her.

Thrusting and grunting like I'm trying to save both of our lives, and maybe I am.

She screams my name, and only my name, and that's more like it.

Tight and wet and mine. Mine to infuriate, mine to please, and mine to empty myself into until all that's left is a groan and her name on my lips and a silent prayer to one day tell her how I really feel. Out loud. Fearlessly. Because it already feels like a lie of omission.

But what's true and good and real right now is this sweet release and the way she holds me tight, cooing and encouraging me to come for her.

And I do.

I come for her.

I come for me.

I come for the man I want to be for her and the us that I always saw us becoming.

The dark, quiet stillness that follows the blast is sweet relief and instant regret at the same time.

Because I can't ask her to stay here with me instead of spending Christmas with her family.

And I can't tell her just how lonely I'll be at the office without her.

And I can't ask her to invite me to her family dinner.

So I say nothing.

She says nothing.

We catch our breaths.

We'll catch our separate flights back to New York.

And I'll keep pretending that it's my brother's wedding that I need Maddie for and not every damn thing that makes my life worth living.

Chapter Twenty-Six

MADDIE: You asshole!!! We said no Christmas presents!
DECLAN: You said no exchanging of Christmas presents. We aren't exchanging gifts. I ordered you something last week, and you did not get anything for me. Who's the asshole now?
MADDIE: <woman facepalming emoji> I didn't want you to feel obligated to get me anything. Did you have Mrs. Pavlovsky put this in here?
DECLAN: Yes. I mean, I had her let the delivery guys in and tell them where to put it. I didn't make an old lady move and set up a punching bag. I'm not that big of an asshole.
MADDIE: Is that why you were looking around my apartment when you came over? To see if I had room for a punching bag?
DECLAN: Sure. I definitely wasn't checking

out all the different surfaces I could fuck you on or against. Wait. This is your personal phone, right?
MADDIE: Well, it's a VERY personal phone now… I will work out so much aggression on this thing. It's really more of a gift for you, but thank you! I love it. Will tape a picture of you to it immediately.
DECLAN: Hey now, I want you to save a little aggression for me.
MADDIE: You back home?
DECLAN: Yep. Getting ready to go to the office. You leaving for your family thing?
MADDIE: In an hour or so. You're really going to the office on Christmas Day?
DECLAN: I've Got My Laws to Keep Me Warm. Get it?… You're really not coming with me?
MADDIE: Tempting. But I mean, I did agree to all this nonsense with you so I could spend time with my family on Christmas, so… <woman shrugging emoji> I'll check up on you later. Don't forget to eat and stuff.
DECLAN: <tumbler of whiskey emoji> Still full. Don't forget to miss me and stuff.
MADDIE: You sure you'll be okay?
DECLAN: I'm always okay.

MADDIE: Hi! Are you really at the office on Christmas? <sad face emoji>
DECLAN: Hi. Miss me already?
MADDIE: OMG yes I totally miss you!!! You and your brother are so hot I can't even believe Eddie Cannavale is your brother you must have the best-looking family in the universe LOL.
DECLAN: Piper, is that you?
MADDIE: Um. No?
DECLAN: Hey, Piper. I'm not mad. And I'm guessing I have the second best-looking family in the universe after yours and Maddie's. <winking face emoji> But Eddie is the ugliest person in mine, poor guy.
MADDIE: ROTFL WOW!!! These pics of you and Eddie are literally the best Christmas presents ever. I can't wait to print them out and wallpaper my room with them. My friends are going to be soooooooo jelly.
DECLAN: Word. You guys eat dinner yet?
MADDIE: Yes but you should come for dessert! I mean, it's not great or anything. I never touch the pumpkin pie, but there's ice cream. Nobody should be alone on Christmas. Have you ever been to Staten Island? It's not as bad as it sounds IMHO.
DECLAN: Maddie didn't invite me, so I probably shouldn't.
MADDIE: She totally wants you here! I heard her tell my mom. My mom was all "Why

didn't you invite him?" and Maddie was like "I didn't think he'd want to come. He's my boss." But you do, right? You're her BAE.
DECLAN: If BAE stands for Bossy Asshole Esquire then yeah. I am.
MADDIE: LOL. Before Anyone Else.
DECLAN: Well, I pay her to put me BAE, so. Doesn't really count.
MADDIE: You should def come. Ima text you Mel's address. Won't tell Maddie in case you don't show up. But you totally should. XO

TWENTY-SEVEN

Maddie

DEC THE HALLS

"Twenty *dollas.* Twenty *dollas* they wanted for a *punkin* at the *punkin* patch in October—I said 'Excuse me? *Excuuuuse* me? Twenty *dollas* for somethin' I'm gonna carve up, stick a candle in, put on the porch so some asshole can kick it to the curb before Halloween is over? Oh my gawd—no thank you. I said 'Where are we—the Hamptons? Do I look like Martha effin' Stewart to you?' I was *appawled. Appaaawwld.* Okay? I'm done. Done with jack-o-lanterns. Twenty *dollas* for somethin' I can't even eat or wear? No thank you. Pass me the Cool Whip from the fridge, will ya, hon? The one that's already open."

I put another dish in the dishwasher and then retrieve one of the sixteen-ounce tubs of Cool Whip from the fridge for my Aunt Mel. She has been complaining about the price of everything from gas to self-tanning spray ever since I got here. One thing she never complains about, though? Christmas decorations from Michaels. Nearly every inch of her house is covered with them. But her Staten Island accent is so cute, Bex and I like to provoke her so she'll keep ranting. "I know, I paid seven dollars for a cup of black coffee at a place on Madison Avenue last month."

"Oh my gawd. Do not even get me started on the price of *cawffee* at those places. Had it up to here with Manhattan ever since Giuliani—I'm done. I been carryin' a thermos of *cawffee* with me everywhere since the nineties, you know this. No shame in it. And what are you even doin' payin' so much for one cup of black *cawffee*—serves you right, hon. You don't wanna carry around a thermos like me, you buy it from a street vendor. A bodega, even. Who are you—a Kardashian? No. Save your money. Okay. I'm takin' this out to the table with the rest of the desserts—it's help yourself, *arright*? Nothin' fancy around here, just eat it if you want it. You know how it goes." She smooths a three-inch layer of whipped topping onto a store-bought pumpkin pie. Nonna Cannavale would shit herself, but I cannot wait to sink my teeth into that thing.

I also can't wait to sink my teeth into Declan Cannavale's butt cheek again. I wanted it, so I took a bite of it. I have never even considered putting my mouth on someone's butt cheek before in my life, but I couldn't stop myself, and I have zero regrets. Piper was right. It's a perfect man butt. I don't know how

I'll ever get enough of that man's body in the next week, but by golly, I'm going to feast on him so hard, it will make last night's dinner look like a Weight Watchers snack.

"Oh my God, just call him and invite him over, why don't you?" I didn't even realize my sister had entered the kitchen or that my aunt had left it. "I know that expression on your face. You're having sex thoughts." She hands me a plate of pumpkin pie and a fork and coughs into her hand, "Maclan!"

"Shhh! Thank you." We both lean against the counter and start shoveling pie into our mouths. "What am I gonna do—have sex with him in the garage while Mom and Dad are watching *It's a Wonderful Life* up here?"

"Hey, you know what they say—YONO!" She waves her fork around in the air.

I laugh so hard I almost spew fake whipped cream everywhere. "It's not YONO. It's YOLO."

"What? I thought it said YONO."

"Where—in Piper's journal?"

"Shhhh!!! What journal—I had no idea my daughter had a journal. I thought it was short for *you never know*. Like you never know what might happen."

"That would be YNK."

"Oh yeah. I just had a baby. Shut up."

"YOLO stands for You Only Live Once."

"Yeah. That too. You only live once." She checks the door to make sure no one's around and whispers, "You don't have to do it in the garage. You can do it on the ferry on the way back." She winks at me and then shoves more pie into her mouth.

"Hah! Right."

Bex waggles her eyebrows. "You wouldn't be the first—all I'm saying."

"Wait—have you done that?"

"My lips are sealed," she says, grinning and nodding. "I promised Josh I wouldn't tell anyone. Which is why I never told you. And I'm not telling you now."

"Nuh-uh! Shut up. You did not!"

Her eyes are practically bulging out of their sockets as she nods vehemently. "No, we would never do that. Especially not last year when we were coming home from Christmas dinner, and you were inside the boat with Piper and Mom and Dad."

"Whaaaaaat? You and Josh did it out on the deck? Come on."

"No, we definitely didn't, because Josh would never do such a thing—and I also didn't give birth to an infant nine months later. I'm just saying—baby it's cold outside, so no one else is around and YOLO. But wear a coat because it really is cold."

I shovel the rest of the pie into my mouth while contemplating this. "I can't bone my boss on the Staten Island Ferry. I mean, he wouldn't even set foot on the Staten Island Ferry."

"What is he—a Kardashian?" she says, imitating my aunt. "Everyone rides the ferry. You already rode your boss in Ohio, so why not give him what every man really wants for Christmas?"

"Public sex while he's freezing his nuts off?"

"Fine then. Don't have sex with him, but invite him over."

"I can't. We can't have dinner with both our families two nights in a row—we aren't actually dating."

"Why are you so afraid of this?"

"Of what? Of ruining this perfectly good temporary fake dating arrangement with my moody boss?"

"Everything's temporary until it isn't. Nothing's real until it is. Every guy you've ever been with 'for real' has been unworthy of you, and you finally have this guy who—"

"I don't have him."

"Please—every relationship you've ever had has ended either because you finally realized the guy was unworthy or because he told you that you deserved better than him, but that always meant he wanted to start seeing someone else. And you do deserve better. You're finally with a guy who's on your level, and you don't even want to admit that it's a thing. I've *seen* the picture. They don't make 'em any better than that. Look at that picture of the two of you on your phone, Maddie. You're a couple."

"Yeah. For six, maybe seven more days. Wait. Where is my phone?" I feel around for my phone, but I don't have any pockets on me right now. "I should probably check in on him. Make sure he ate dinner." I find my phone in my coat pocket, on the bed in my aunt's guest room. I see that there's a missed call from Declan and call him back.

He answers immediately and hesitantly. "Piper?"

I burst out laughing. "Um. No. Would you like to speak with her—who shall I say is calling?"

"JK LOL. How's it going?"

"Fine. How are you? You sound cold. Are you outside?"

"Yeah. I'm just…walking around."

"Where? By your office?"

"Not really. You having fun with your family?"

"Yeah, they're great. It's nice. The baby's so cute, but he's asleep right now. You sound hungry. Did you eat dinner?"

"Not really."

"Dec. You haven't eaten all day?"

"I was working. By myself. I forgot."

Ohhhh fuck it. YOLO.

"Do you want to come over? I mean, we're done eating dinner, but there's plenty of leftovers and dessert. I know it's not part of the plan. What you planned. For us. I mean you and me for the…as part of the…what we discussed before about…" *Holy shit, am I stammering? I'm stammering. I do not stammer. Pull it together, Cooper.* "It's really low-key and very Staten Island, but you're welcome to join us if you don't have anything else to…" I pause because I hear a police siren going by the house outside, and at the same time, I hear a siren through the phone.

"You sure you want me to meet your family? I don't want to impose."

I shuffle over to the living room, past my family who are watching *Love Actually* on a gigantic big screen TV, and peek out the window. "Oh my gawd," I whisper into the phone as I stare out at my boss down on the sidewalk, all bundled up in a puffy coat, scarf, and beanie.

"What is it?" my aunt calls out from the sofa. "Is my neighbor throwin' his trash in my bins again? I swear to gawd this time I'll kill him."

"Dec," I say into the phone. "What are you doing here?"

"OMG, is he here?!" Piper jumps up and runs over to the window next to me.

"Is who here?" My sister comes over to look.

My niece's hands shoot up in the air as she does a victory dance. "It's Declan! He's out front! I gave him the address, and he came!"

"Gave who the address? Who's Declan?" My mother gets up from the sofa to join us. "Dad—pause the movie!"

"Where is everyone going all of a sudden?" my dad asks. "This is my favorite part of the entire film."

When Declan looks up from the street, he sees my whole family and me peering out the window at him excitedly, like he's Santa Claus and we're all finding out he's real after all these years of being cynics.

"Well, I was in the neighborhood…" he finally says. "There appears to be a group of people staring at me through a window."

"That's us. Come inside."

"Okay, but what did you tell them about us? About me?"

"Everything. They know everything," I say, and then I hang up.

"You guys—that's my new boss and I'm pretending to be his girlfriend over the holidays, but don't make a big deal about it. Okay?"

I look back out the window and watch Declan slide his phone into his jacket pocket, carrying a shopping bag, as he crosses the street to walk up the driveway. It's dark out, and he's lit by a nearby streetlamp, but you can still see, plain as day, that he's the best-looking guy on Staten Island right now.

"Oh, he's very good-looking," my mother says.

"Wait till you see his butt!" Piper exclaims.

"You're only pretending for the holidays?" my mom asks. "What then?"

"Good question, Mom," my sister says. "What then, Maddie?"

I wave them both off. "It's just for the holidays. Everybody behave!"

"What is happening? Maddie, do you have a boyfriend? Is your boyfriend comin' inside?" My aunt fusses with her hair and apron and starts skittering about. "Aw shit! I wasn't expectin' company."

"What are you talking about? *We're* company," my dad says.

"I mean *male* company."

"What are we, chopped liver?" Bex's husband asks.

"Basically." Bex plops down on his lap, kisses his cheek, and then steals a bite of his Rice Krispy treat, and they are so cute together it hurts. What they have, it's secretly all I've ever really wanted. Even before I knew about the ferry sex.

"Oh calm down, Mel!" my mom yells as she frantically straightens up the pillows on all of the sofas and armchairs in my aunt's living room. "The place looks terrific. What man doesn't love being surrounded by bargain-priced glittery Christmas ornaments and starfish with Santa hats? Especially lawyers?"

"Yeah," Piper says without any irony whatsoever. "You've got a cute stuffed raccoon in a wool cap and scarf on the mantle. He'll love it! But Declan will only have eyes for Maddie anyway."

I grab that kid's sweet face and kiss her on the top of her head before going to the door to pull my boots on.

"Don't let him in yet!" my aunt shrieks. "It smells like roast chicken farts in here! Open a window! Open all of the windows!"

My dad and brother-in-law point at each other, and I crack open a window because she's not wrong. But all houses smell like that at holiday dinners, right? If Declan can't deal with my family's chicken farts, then he can just go straight back to the office.

I open the front door and step out onto the porch, hugging myself tight and jogging in place. Not because it's cold as fuck but because my heart is racing, and I have so much nervous energy I feel like I could outrun the Polar Express right now. This is so unlike me, but these past few days have been unlike anything I've ever experienced or imagined myself. There isn't even anything fairy tale romantic or extraordinary about it, and that's what makes it even more surreal.

Declan Cannavale is walking up the driveway to my aunt's house. Where my family is gathered. In Staten Island. And I didn't have to get him to sign a contract or offer a few days off in return, either. Talk about a Christmas miracle.

I wait for him to walk up the steps, and then I do the dumbest thing yet—I hold my hand out to shake his.

He stares at my outstretched hand for a second and then says, "Oh. Okay."

I had my mouth on his penis this morning, and now it feels awkward to hug him, so this is what's happening.

Declan Cannavale has broken my brain.

"Nice to see you. Happy Christmas," he says like an uptight British guy.

I swat at his hand. "Oh shut up. I'm nervous."

"That's adorable. I'm not. At all." I can tell he is, though. He totally is, and we're so fucking cute I want to hug both of us.

But I don't.

"Whatcha got there?" I nod at the bag in his hand.

"I had the driver drop me off at a gift shop," he says, shrugging and grinning. He holds up a plastic bag from a souvenir and gift shop on Fifth Avenue, and I want to French kiss that dimple on his stubbly cheek. But not in front of my dad.

"You got my family New York souvenirs. That's

funny." I hold my hand up for a high-five. "That is really cute."

"Well, I'm fucking adorable, so what'd you expect?"

We just stand here, staring at each other and grinning like goofballs for a minute.

"Hi," he says, pushing a strand of hair out of my face.

"Hi." I rub the scruff on the sides of his face. I think this is how happy I would have felt if I'd actually gotten the puppy I wanted for Christmas when I was eight, except this puppy has a law degree and looks like an underwear model. Goddammit. My heart feels so full right now. And the rest of me is horny. Really, really horny. "So you have a car?"

"I was drinking a bit earlier, so I had someone drive me here. Sent him back though. I wasn't sure how you wanted to go back to the city. I mean, assuming you wanted to go back to the city tonight. With me."

"I do. We're taking the ferry. We should go inside now."

"Yep. Let's do this."

I take his hand to lead him inside. Not because he's my fake boyfriend but because I do it without thinking. And I'm not even going to think about what that means. I open the door and peek inside to find Mel running around spritzing apple cider–scented bathroom spray like a maniac.

"Mel! The house smells fine! We're coming in!"

I pull Declan into the living room, and we're met

with my family's wide-eyed, sheepish faces and silence because my mom made my dad pause *Love Actually* again. So all I can hear is the beating of my very confused heart and the train set that's going around my aunt's fake Christmas tree.

"Hi there," Declan says, surveying the room. "I like that raccoon. I have a scarf just like his."

TWENTY-EIGHT

Declan

HAVE YOURSELF A STATEN ISLAND FERRY CHRISTMAS

It took Hannah three months to convince me to go home with her to meet her parents on Thanksgiving back when we were in college. At that point, we'd been dating for almost a year. Granted, I was nineteen and a total shit, but it felt like a really big deal, and it was. We had our first real relationship-y fights about it. She wanted to meet my family too. I also met that request with all of the resistance of a nineteen-year-old total shit. But we did finally do the family holiday thing. That made the relationship feel more real to me. I felt more like a grown-up. All it really was, was the first time Hannah had met Brady. I thought it was the beginning of something, and it was. Not for me but for them.

It took three days, six lonely hours at the office, four fingers of whiskey, and a text from a thirteen-year-old to convince me to come meet Maddie's family. And while it may be significant for a thirty-two-year-old semi-shit to do this, I think that I would do anything for Maddie right now if she asked me to. And that would have been true even after only two fingers of whiskey.

I mean, I'm the king of gift-giving, and I got her parents a fucking New York City snow globe. As an inside joke between Maddie and me. I look like an ass. But I don't care because Maddie gets the joke. I was not, however, expecting Maddie's Aunt Mel to be so excited about the creepy Nutcracker doll that I got for half off. There must be a bare three-inch square space of surface somewhere in this house that she's been saving for something just like it.

"Oh get out of here, *mistah*! Hello—did you read my mind?" she says, giving my shoulder a shove. "Mistah Readin' My Mind over here gets me a *Nutcrackah* doll after I'm thinkin' for a month—you know what this place needs? A *Nutcrackah* doll! This is goin' somewhere special, but I'm puttin' it here on the table for now, *arright*? You hungry, hon? I'm gonna fix you a plate. I'll get you a plate of everythin'. It'll be reheated, nothin' fancy. Just *whatevah*."

"Yeah whatever. That'd be great, thanks."

"Okay, hon, make yourself comfortable, sit. Eh, Joe!" she yells out to Maddie's father who is six feet away. "Joe, let our guest sit by you there, on the good sofa." She waves at him to make room for me while pushing me toward him.

So I guess I'm sitting next to Mr. Cooper on the

good sofa, instead of standing behind the armchair next to Maddie. She looks so wholesome in her big chunky sweater and those tight black things—leggings, I think my sister called them—and she seems so nervous. I want to stick my hands up that sweater, pull those leggings down, and help her relax a little. Or a lot. But maybe not in front of her family.

"Have a seat—Declan, is it?"

"Declan, yes." It really is a good sofa, but because Maddie's brother-in-law and sister are also sitting on it, I have to nestle into the corner, uncomfortably close to Joe Cooper. We're basically rubbing up against each other on one side.

Colin Firth is paused on a massive screen, and it looks like he's about to sneeze.

"You seen this movie before? *Love Actually*? It's British. A classic British romantic comedy film."

"I've seen parts of it, whenever it's on TV."

"Parts of it, huh? Interesting. Too busy working to watch entire movies?"

"To be honest, yeah. I was. But I'm trying to make some changes in my life now."

I'm not even going to think about what it means that I'm saying this shit to get Maddie's dad to like me within minutes of meeting him.

"Yeah? By pretending to be my daughter's boyfriend?"

"Well…"

"I'm just fucking with you. That sounds like a perfectly normal thing to do." He gives me a reassuring wink.

"Really?"

"No. It's messed up. But you must have your reasons. And you didn't come to Christmas dinner wearing cargo shorts and knee socks, so I guess I'd rather she pretended to be your girlfriend than have her actually date more of those losers with the bad socks."

"Dad!" Maddie rubs her temples. "That was senior year of high school!"

"Nothing worse than bad socks." I casually lift up the cuffs of my pants so he can see the Italian-made socks Nonna gave me this year.

He pats me on the shoulder. "Good socks." Then he aims the remote at the TV and un-pauses the movie. "Watch the movie. This is my favorite part."

So I watch the last half of *Love Actually* with Maddie's family and eat a reheated mash-up of like nine different kinds of food that I never get to eat at Christmas, and it's all good, and I love it. I love it so much that I barely even think about how hard it will suck when I inevitably screw this up.

It's not until the cab drops Maddie and me off outside the Staten Island Ferry terminal that I finally say to her, "So when you said you told your family 'everything' about us, you meant..."

"The faking thing. Not the sex."

"Got it." I put my arm around her waist and bring her in closer to me because it's freezing and because I've been in a room with her and her family for two hours, and I just need to touch her. Even if it's over a big puffy coat and a big chunky sweater. "So not the part about you biting my ass this morning."

She snort-laughs and looks around to see if anyone heard that. No one heard. No one else is around. It's freezing, it's Christmas, and it's nine thirty at night. I don't know how I'm going to wait until we get back to my place to get my hands under that sweater and get those leggings off her, but I'll have to. "Shhh! I mean, I tweeted about it, but my family doesn't follow me so it's fine."

We get inside the terminal, and I can see that she's blushing, and it's so fucking cute. Never in my wildest dreams did I expect to see Maddie Cooper blushing. Never in my filthiest fantasies about her did I imagine myself stopping to kiss her on her forehead on Staten Island. But that's what's happening.

I don't even want to think about what it means that just pressing my lips against her forehead makes me a little stiff. And more than that even. It makes me want to take her home, make her a mug of hot chocolate, and curl up in front of the fireplace with her. After I fuck her like a maniac three or four times first.

"You ever ride the Staten Island Ferry before?" she asks, and I can tell by her tone that she already knows the answer.

"I have not yet had the pleasure, but I've heard great things. There really aren't enough orange boats in the world."

She elbows me in the ribs, and I barely feel it

because we both have so much padding between us, which is terrible.

"It's actually really stunning to see the Statue of Liberty from the water."

"Oh well, I've done that. From a yacht."

"Oh *whatevah, mistah*," she says.

And now I'm more than a little stiff.

"Keep talking like that."

"Like this? You like it when I *tawk* about how I spend eight *dollahs* on a cup of *cawffee*? You like that?"

"Yeah, baby, I like it a lot."

"Oh my gawd." She stops to look me in the face, very serious. "Are you really turned-on right now?"

"My *cawk* is *hawd* as a fuckin' teenage *rawk* right now."

"Me too. I mean I'm really turned-on right now too." Suddenly, she pulls away from me and looks around the terminal. "Shit, I forgot someone from work could see us."

"Right... Work." I shove my hands into my pockets. *Right. I'm a lawyer. And she's the best assistant I've ever had. Right...* "Fuck it," I say, grabbing her and dipping her. "It's Christmas." I plant a kiss on her the likes of which Staten Island has never seen before. I feel her arms around my neck, her body relaxing into my embrace, and Colin Firth can kiss my delicious American ass—I'm romantic as fuck.

When I finally pull my mouth away from hers and lift her up, her eyelashes flutter magnificently and then her eyes close. "You mean that?" she whispers.

"As an attorney, I would never joke about a potentially hazardous situation with an employee, even when it's regarding non-work activities," I quote myself back to her, and she laughs.

"Fucking lawyers," she says, shaking her head.

"Fucking right."

"Do you *really* want to throw caution to the wind on this cold, cold night, Mr. Cannavale? Come what may?"

I take her gloved hand in mine. "Come what may."

Ten minutes later, we're on the boat and Maddie's pulling her gloves off, shoving them into her pockets and telling me to remove my gloves too as she leads me through the cabin to one of the doors to an upper deck. It's colder than a dead elf's balls outside, but I will follow her anywhere because I have a feeling something awesome is about to happen. She calmly surveys the deck before pulling me through the heavy metal door. There aren't a lot of people inside on this level, and there's no one else out on the deck, but there are windows everywhere. She leans back against a tall metal gate right beside the door, inhales deeply as she unzips her long coat, removes her boots, and pulls her leggings and panties off.

"Be quick," she says, unzipping my coat.

"I think you're great" is all I can say, before her mouth is on mine, and I'm getting my hands all up under that sweater. She's unzipping my pants, and right before my lawyer brain shuts down, I remind myself that as long as none of our private parts are exposed, we can't be charged for indecent exposure, so that leaves the "lewd act" misdemeanor, and I could argue that we're in a secluded area, but yeah. I'll be quick.

There's no time for fondling. I will stand and deliver. She curls one leg up around me, tilting her hips so I can push inside her, and we both groan so loud because *fuck*. She's so warm and wet, and not one part of me is cold right now. I grab her by the ass, lift her up, and she wraps both legs around my waist. The metal gate provides a kind of industrial percussion beat as her back slams against it with every thrust.

She carries her own weight as much as she can, one hand clasped around my neck, one behind my head. Her head drops back, and I get one look at that face, and I can't stop my mouth from releasing every dirty thing that I held back this morning. "Goddammit, Maddie. You are the sexiest fucking woman I have ever known. The first time I saw you I wanted to make you scream my name and come all over you."

"Dec. Yes. Fuck."

"You drive me crazy, you know?"

"Yes. I like it…"

I like that she likes it, and I can't stop myself from ramming into her extra hard, just once. She curses and squeezes her legs around me tighter, and I can feel her starting to contract and release around me already and I'm delirious. "You own my cock, you know that?"

"Yes. I want it."

"It's yours." I don't even know how I can perform like this after eating, much less talk while fucking, but *ding dong merrily I'm high* on adrenaline and lust for this woman. "What about your pussy?"

"Yours."

"It's mine."

"Yes."

"All mine."

"Yes. So good. The way we fit."

"No one will ever fuck you the way I do."

"No one ever has. Dec. Oh my God." Her climax comes hard and fast and beautiful, and I want to live in this crazy moment as much as I want to live in every other moment I've spent with her over the past few days. I don't even want to think about what that means. Because I can't.

All I have is this. The freezing cold air around us, the heat between us, and the frantic, terrible dilemma of wanting to come and wanting to make this last forever. She arches her back and then presses herself against me, changing angles. And those tiny movements are all it takes to put me over the edge as she takes me with her. Overboard. Into her. Out of my mind. Right up against the only woman on earth who could open me up completely or shut me down for good.

I know better than to call an orgasm love, but I've never had to fight the urge to say that word out loud to someone I'm having sex with before. It already feels wrong, not saying it to the woman who brought me back to life and kept me on track, even before I got to see her naked. Even on the deck of the Staten Island Ferry on Christmas.

Her whole body is wrapped around mine, arms around my neck, chin resting on my shoulder, legs around my waist but hidden under my coat. I can't catch my breath, but I can see it. I can feel her heart beating against my chest, and I want her to tell me that it's mine, but that's not dirty talk. It's the kind of straight talk that I can't engage in, as her boss, as an attorney, or as a man who is on the cusp of becoming the man who actually deserves Maddie Cooper.

I let her down easy and bend down to retrieve her panties and leggings. But before she pulls them on, I slip a glove onto my right hand and wipe myself off from between her legs. She gasps when I do it. It's not a sex gasp, it's a *holy shit I can't believe you're doing that for me* gasp, and it's just as satisfying. There's so much I want to do for her, and it scares me. I don't want to be scared of it because she deserves better than a man who is afraid of his feelings for her. But I can do this for her now, so I will.

I wipe myself off too, remove the glove before folding it up and putting it back in my pocket. I'll deal with that and so many other things later. We're now fully dressed again, and we may look freshly fucked, but there's no law against that.

I take her face in my hands and kiss her parted lips. The tip of her nose is cold, but her mouth is warm and her tongue is warm, and we should probably go back inside the cabin before I whip my dick out again. A soft, appreciative moan comes from deep in her throat as she kisses me. Sweet and sexy as hell. She is all these things and so much more, and I want them as much as I always did.

I just don't know what to do with this totally unfamiliar and completely unexpected feeling in my chest and in the pit of my stomach.

I got a hot and surprisingly wonderful fake girlfriend for the holidays, but I lost my cocky shithead attitude somewhere back in Youngstown. I don't miss being a cocky shithead—well, maybe a little—but there's a river of doubt that's a lot wider than the New York Harbor separating me from the place that I want to get to with Maddie.

She pulls away from me, slowly, and I look down at her. I should say something. Aren't I the guy who always knows what to say? As always, she saves me from myself by staring over my shoulder and saying, "Look."

I turn to see the Statue of Liberty. Glowing and majestic. A beacon of hope and opportunity for weary travelers. The goddess of liberty before me, a goddess of sex and executive administrative skills and potentially a domestic goddess that I would shack up with right behind me.

"Your place or mine?" she asks, wrapping her arms around my waist and pressing her cheek against my back.

"Anywhere. Long as I'm with you," I say. I say it out loud because *fuck you, Colin Firth—I can have hot quick and dirty sex on a ferry* and *say cheesy things without laughing.*

It doesn't stop Maddie from laughing at me and burying her face into my coat. But it's cool. One day she'll figure out that I mean everything I say to her. And one day I'll be able to say everything I want to say to her. I just hope it'll be before we ring in the new year.

TWENTY-NINE

Maddie

FAIRLY DARK ALE OF NEW YORK

BEX: Well? Did you rock the boat last night or what?
ME: I would NEVER tell you or anyone else if we did it against a metal gate on the upper deck. Or that it was super-hot and surprisingly romantic. Because everyone involved is way too classy for that kind of thing. <winking face emoji>
BEX: <raising hands emoji> YOLO!!! See?!?! It pays to take your big sister's advice every now and then. You at home?
ME: At his place, actually.
BEX: Wow. Sounds serious.
ME: It's not. It's just, you know. For now. But his apartment is incredible, and these sheets are amazing.

BEX: Are you texting me while you're in bed with him? If so, your relationship is progressing a little too rapidly IMHOP.
ME: <laughing face emoji> It's IMHO. <face with rolling eyes emoji> He left a note that he went out to pick up breakfast. He's being so sweet. It's deeply annoying.
BEX: Yeah, that sucks. Josh and I spent the night in Mel's guest room with the baby and the life-size glow in the dark nativity scene and the roast chicken farts. But your thing sounds way more annoying. <raised middle finger emoji>
ME: Oh shit. I think he's back. We didn't do it on the ferry, so never discuss this with anyone ever again, including me! xo
BEX: Roger that. Josh is dropping Piper off at her friend's house, so obviously I WON'T be reading her journals while tidying up her room now. xo

I stretch and slide out of Declan's bed, yawning. So much for my "No Sleepovers" rule. According to my phone, it is almost eleven, and I don't think I've slept in this late since I was a teenager. But I only got about five hours sleep. My lips feel swollen, the skin all over my body is pink from being thoroughly exfoliated by holiday scruff, and let's just say that I will not be riding a bike today because things are a little tender down there. But happy. Deliriously, terrifyingly happy.

There's a large gray men's T-shirt laid out on top

of the covers of my side of the bed, along with a pair of boxer briefs and wool socks. There's a Post-it note on the boxer briefs that says ***previously unworn***. As if I wouldn't slip on a pair of Declan Cannavale's previously worn undies after becoming so intimate with the part of his body that he wears them on. So thoughtful. So annoying.

So wrong?

I shake that concept off, slip into his clothes, and pad into the kitchen, where Declan's plating our take-out breakfast and placing it on bed trays. I've never been with a guy who owned a bed tray before. Much less two of them.

That's when I realize he probably lived here with Hannah and that she's probably the one who bought them. I wonder how many other women he's made breakfast in bed for. I inhale the most tantalizing coffee aroma and wonder how it's possible that the man I've bought coffee for every weekday morning as per his request can make coffee himself at home.

When he sees me, he holds a croissant midair and does a slow, full sweep of me from head to toe and back up again. The grin that spreads across his face is as handsome and inviting as his apartment, and they both belong on the cover of a magazine. But I'm not ready to share either of them with the rest of the world again yet.

"Morning," I say, grinning back and smoothing the soft fabric of his T-shirt over my body.

He has to clear his throat before saying, "Hey…"

And now my day has been made. "I was going to bring you breakfast in bed."

"Would you like me to get back in your bed?"

"Is that a trick question?"

I spot a large, gorgeous flower arrangement on the kitchen counter, and it definitely wasn't there when he fucked me on it last night. "Wow. Dec. Those are gorgeous. Did you get those when you went out to pick up the food?"

"Yeah. You think Mrs. P will like them?" He sucks butter off his thumb, and I'm pretty sure I remember a time when I couldn't decide if that smirk made me want to slap or kiss him, but I have this strange urge to create another tiny person with those dimples and those shiny golden brown eyes.

I have to shake that concept off too. "Mrs. Pavlovsky? You bought more flowers for my landlady?"

"You got a problem with that? She's my girl."

"You planning on having more boxing equipment delivered to my apartment when I'm not there?"

"Sometimes I just like to give women flowers, Magdalena." He crosses over to the table by the front door and holds up an elegant orchid plant in a gold patina vessel. "This is for you."

"Dec, that's gorgeous. I love orchids."

"I know. It's for your desk."

Right. My desk. At the office. Where we work together. And he's my bossy boss who bosses me around, day and night.

"Thank you," I finally remember to say. "That's very thoughtful of you."

"And I definitely didn't imagine bending you over your desk and fucking you while I was paying for this. Because that would be a clear violation of the company's current nonfraternization policy. But I have it on good authority that the in-house attorney will be officially rewriting said policy tomorrow. So keep that desk clear." He gives me an exaggerated wink. But not even that dimple can subdue the oncoming dread that's even worse than what I felt when I was a kid who didn't want to go back to school after Christmas break.

He puts his hands on my hips and presses his lips to my forehead, and okay, maybe it's not as bad as going back to school. Because I never went to school with anyone as hot and charming as Declan Cannavale.

"Let's go back to bed," he says. "I've never used those trays before."

Declan miraculously finds a parking space right in front of my apartment building in the early afternoon, and by now I'm not anxious about anything anymore because we showered together. And by "showered together," I mean we had sex in his big amazing shower. Mrs. Pavlovsky is sweeping the stoop, and I know she's a seventy-year-old widow who still loves her deceased husband and all, but from the way she's looking at Declan as he approaches her with an arm full of flowers, I'm pretty sure she'd let him bone her on a ship if he was into it.

"Ohhh, *vat* is *zis*? For me?"

"For you," he says, giving her a gentle hug before handing her the bouquet like she's a prima ballerina.

"*Sank* you. Ohhh, *zis* man, Magdalena! You see? I say to you before—put more fat on bones and good man *vill* come. *Zis* is good man for you!"

Aww. Mrs. P. Your heart is going to be broken in January. "Seems to me he's a good man for *you*, Madame Pavlovsky."

"Ohhh! Psssh!" She waves off that thought and then puts her hand on Declan's coat. "Not for me, no. *Zis* is a—how you say? Flirtation." She rolls the "r" like it's a run-on sentence and it's lovely. A flirtation with Mr. Boss Butt *would* be lovely. Although I suppose that's what we had before the holidays.

"There ya go," Declan says, patting her hand, which is still grasping on to his coat. "We're gonna grab a drink at McSorley's. You want to come?"

"Ohhhh nooo! Nooo, not for me. You go! You go! Don't let me keep you, young people. Come by for some *kutya* later, yes? Good. Yes." She finally lets go of Declan and beams at us, clutching the flowers to her chest as she watches us walk down to the pub—not hand-in-hand, not bumping shoulders.

Just walking down a sidewalk like two people who didn't totally just go down on each other under a vigorous stream of water forty minutes ago. Maybe this is how it will be at the office. Maybe he was right when he said we're just a couple of straightforward hot as fuck people who can handle vacation sex and then go back to business as usual. Maybe it is just the holidays stirring up emotions, the isolated period of time in which we've been interacting with each other in more casual environments than we're accustomed to. I hate that I can remember every single thing he's ever said to me, and I hope I can forget every appallingly wonderful sexy thing he's said to me the past few days.

Declan holds the door to McSorley's Old Ale House and leans in to say in my ear as I pass by, "I really wanted to hold your hand just now, FYI."

Goddammit. I'll never forget that he said that.

"Me too."

The pub is barely a quarter full of patrons. It's early afternoon the day after Christmas, so I'm not surprised. They still have the strings of lights and minimal Christmas décor up, and the holiday music is still playing. I'm glad. I'm certainly not ready for this part of the year to be over.

"Mug or glass?" he asks me.

"Fuck it—mug. I'll get a table in the back."

"I like your style, kid."

I take the table for four in the back part of the bar, just inside the door behind the wall so we're secluded. I've never run into anyone from work in my neighborhood, but you never know. Real estate brokers get around all over town.

Declan places two mugs of dark ale on the table and takes the chair next to mine.

"To not letting this interfere with our fantastic work relationship," I say as we clink glasses. "Come what may."

He gets a glint in his eye, and I already know he's going to hit me with his Irish accent again dammit. "May your mornings bring joy and your evenings bring peace. May your troubles grow less as your blessings increase."

God, I love it when he talks dirty to me.

"May no one walk in on you when you're dancing around naked to 'Come and Get Your Love'—unless you want them to." I raise my glass and then take a big gulp.

"May you only walk in on naked dancers as hot as I am." We clink glasses again and take another sip.

I hold the mug up again and say, "May your nonna's heart always be as soft and warm as her meatballs."

"May your aunt's accent always be as thick as her mashed *potatuhs, arright?*"

"May the only teeth in your ass belong to the woman you're banging."

He almost does a spit take at that one. He wipes his mouth with the back of his hand. "Well, I never."

We stare at each other, smiling like goofballs again. I bring the mug to my lips and take a big gulp of ale to prevent myself from saying anything that might actually articulate these feelings I'm having. I might have to instill another "no talking rule" for the rest of the day. And I definitely think we should sleep at separate apartments tonight.

But I don't get the chance to bring any of this up because The Pogues' song "Fairytale of New York" comes on, and a reverent hush comes over all of the twenty or so customers in the pub, followed by everyone raising their glasses and singing along.

"I fecking love this song," Declan muses just before the music picks up and Kirsty MacColl joins in.

We sing this beautiful, messy underdog Christmas anthem duet to each other like a couple of drunk college kids. If I did a graph of how happy I've ever allowed myself to be with Declan, this would be the pinnacle. He's singing with his entire body and being, and I wish I could have been the one who met him in college instead of Hannah. When he was still made of youthful energy and optimism.

Or maybe I don't.

Maybe I prefer him this way—moody survivor of a broken heart and full of surprises.

"Ahhh, it's a grand old song," he says, shaking his head as the song ends. "You ever been to Ireland?"

"No. Have you?"

"Oh sure." He gets a faraway look in his eyes and places his hand over his heart. It looks like he's about to recite a William Butler Yeats poem or something, but instead he says something even more romantic: "I'd love to take you there someday. Italy too."

The tip of my nose is tingling, and the rims of my eyes are stinging, and I take a deep breath because I'm finally going to say something real.

"Maddie! I *thought* you lived around here!" I look

up and see Cindy, the receptionist from Sentinel, walking out from the restrooms, only it takes me a few seconds to recognize her, all bundled up in her winter coat and accessories.

"Cindy! Hi." I stand up to hug her. "What are you doing in these parts?"

"Oh, I was just on my way to my friend's place on the Lower East Side, and I had to pee, so I stopped in for a quick glass of ale." She finally sees Declan sitting in the chair next to mine. "Oh! Hi, Mr. Cannavale! I'm so sorry—I didn't see you there. Happy holidays!"

He stands up to hug her just as she holds her hand out to shake his. "Happy holidays," he says.

"Oh!" She gasps and wraps her arms around him. "Thank you."

"Can I get you another beer?" he asks casually. "Would you like to join us?"

"Thank you, no, I'm already late for my friend."

Both Declan and Cindy are watching me. It feels like my right eye is twitching. "Declan just dropped off my belated Christmas gift, so I invited him for a quick drink," I explain. "I live right by here."

"Right," she says. "That's great."

"*Right.*" Declan looks down at the table. "Welp. Since I'm up, I'll hit the jacks real quick. Excuse me." He pats Cindy on the shoulder and heads to the doors that lead to the restrooms.

Cindy and I watch him go. He's wearing dark jeans, and his butt looks magnificent in them.

"You don't have to worry about me saying anything to anyone at work, Maddie." Cindy touches my arm, reassuring me. "My friends and I go out a lot during the day on weekends, all over town, and you wouldn't believe how many people I've seen together from the office. All hungover and post-coital. But don't ask who, because I won't tell." She mimes locking her lips and throwing away the key.

"Really? Wow. That's an effective policy, huh? But really, this isn't anything."

"Hmmm. Not what it looks like to me, but if you say so. Okay. Say goodbye to Mr. Cannavale for me. Got any big plans for New Year's?"

"Not really," I say with a shrug. Another lie. "You?"

She grins. "Huge." She waggles her eyebrows and waves as she walks away. "See ya."

I sit back down and finish my beer. My ears are ringing, and this dark ale tastes more bitter than it did a minute ago. When I see the expression on Declan's face as he returns to the table, I feel guilty for making up that lie. Being around all those Catholics, their guilt has rubbed off on me or something.

"Hi," I say when he sits down opposite me.

"Hey."

"I'm sorry I made up that dumb lie. I guess I panicked."

"Wasn't dumb at all. It's what I would have said too. You're such a good liar. You'd make a good lawyer." He raises his nearly empty mug. "May all your lies be laced with truth and your truths laced with whiskey." He twists his lips to the side and shrugs. "Or something a lot cleverer than that."

I'm about to say what I wanted to say before we started singing, but he slams the mug down on the table, stands, and blurts out, "Should we head to your place? Or maybe I should go home?" There's that mood again. And here I thought we were done with all that.

"No. Come to my place. I want you to."

"You sure?"

"You're coming to my place, Dec. You *vill* have some kutya. And you *vill* like it."

He gets a flash of something in his eyes—horniness, I guess, but I'll take it. I'll take it day-by-day with him, and we'll see where that leads us. Even if it leads to disappointment or worse by January first. At least we'll have tonight.

THIRTY

Declan

DO YOU FEAR WHAT I FEAR?

This has been the best post-Christmas hangover I've ever had. I've always thought of the hazy period between the 26th and 30th of December as the taint of the holiday season. It ain't Christmas and it ain't New Year's Eve. But Maddie Cooper has found the sweet spot, gently massaged it, and stimulated it to the point where I now think of it as the exciting climax.

I can't seem to stop waiting for the other shoe to drop, though. I had thought that seeing Brady and Hannah together and finally forgiving them was enough. I thought being truly happy with someone for once in my life was enough. I'm still a fucking badass alpha and all, but if I'm this happy with this woman, it might just kill me if she leaves me. And I'm the idiot who created this weird situation to begin with. This is what they call a fool's paradise. I'm not the kind of guy who's comfortable being the fool, but I'm not ready to leave here yet and I don't regret getting us here either.

It seemed like the only logical thing to do at the time. Or maybe logic never really came into play. Regardless, I don't want to lose her as an assistant, and I don't want to lose her as a girlfriend. I want all of it to be real, and I want all of it to last. I just need to show her that things can go back to the way they were between us at work when we're still involved outside the office. I'll talk to Shapiro and HR as soon as the holidays are over if that's what she wants.

It's what I want.

We've been spending entire days and nights at each other's apartments since the 26th, and she somehow managed to convince me to stay away from the office all that time. Running into the receptionist put a damper on our spirits for maybe ten minutes. I didn't love that Maddie's go-to response was to lie, but I get it. We decided not to take any more chances, and we've been in our own little world since then. We haven't killed each other yet, so I'm optimistic.

She went home to change clothes after breakfast at my place today, and I convinced her to join me at the office because I have a shit-ton of calls and emails to return and half a shit-ton of contracts to go over. She wanted to drive to Sentinel separately so she can leave to visit her sister at some point. So I'm on my way there, and I've already let two assholes cut in front of me because I'm in such a good mood.

Another car in another lane is signaling, and you know what—I'm gonna let him in ahead of me too. I slow down and gesture for him to go ahead. The car behind me honks, and I don't even flip him off. That's how good I feel about the world right now. So good that I decide to accept a call from Brady on my personal phone. Even though I know he's probably with my cousins right now because they flew into Cleveland yesterday, and they've all been drunk texting me since last night. I put him on speaker phone and answer with: "You got a hangover or are you still drunk?"

"Haaa! I knew you'd *ansah* if I used your *bruthah's* phone. 'Sup, Manhattan?" It's my cousin Billy O'Sullivan from Boston.

"'Sup, Billy Boy. You steal Brady's phone?"

"Nah, he left it chargin' in the *cah*. He's out there pickin' up some kinda weddin' *whatevah* for Hannah around town. Givin' us a ride back to the hotel. We all had breakfast *togethah* at your *mutha's*. You gettin' in today or what?"

"I'll get in tomorrow afternoon for the bachelor thing. I've got work to do. I'm on my way to the office right now."

"Aww, come on! You think you're *bettah* than us? Bang out and get your ass *ovah heah*, ya fuckin' skeezah. Eddie's not comin' in till *tamorrah eithah*. It's just us and these married guys. I hear you got a girlfriend now—what *ah* ya, pussy-whipped?"

I hear a guy in the background say, "Lemme talk to that fecker." It's Nolan, my other single cousin, from Ireland. He'll play the good cop with me now, but he's the one who's never satisfied until all of his

American relatives have alcohol poisoning. "Declan! How ya getting on? Thanks fer replying to my texts, ya gobshite."

"I definitely responded to one of them."

"Yeah yeah, really big of ya. Listen, it's grand that you got yourself a fine thing now, and we're all happy for ya what with your brother riding Hannah all year. But we're here to celebrate Brady getting married, eh? So bunk off, bring the bird, and get yer arse over here."

"I will definitely do that tomorrow."

They both curse me, and I hear the car door open and my brother's voice. "Hey. Who are you calling?... Dec? Are they giving you shit for not being here? Don't even worry about it—you've got work to do. I can handle them until tomorrow."

"It definitely sounds like you've got it under control over there."

He whispers into the phone, "Help me, bro. Aiden and Casey are no fucking use to me, and Eddie won't be here until tomorrow. I'll be dead by sundown if you aren't here as a buffer."

"I feel for you, Brady, I do. But I have so much work to catch up on. I'll see you tomorrow, I promise."

"Don't even sweat it—we'll see you tomorrow."

I hear Billy yell out "*cocksuckah*" right before he hangs up. I'm a shit brother. I do love the guy, but he did start riding my ex right after we broke up, and I really have a lot of work to catch up on.

. . .

They still haven't taken down the Christmas decorations at the Sentinel corporate offices yet, and the building's still piping in cheesy canned holiday music, but it doesn't bother me anymore. I nod at the temp receptionist when I walk off the elevator and say, "Morning. Happy holidays." She looks really surprised because I didn't say anything to her when I saw her on Christmas Day. Because on Christmas Day, I knew I wouldn't be seeing Maddie Cooper at her desk. Today I will. And even though I won't be doing anything unprofessional to her on that desk, today will be a good day. As long as the other shoe doesn't drop.

It looks like there are a few other random people working today, or maybe they just don't have anywhere better to be. What's-his-name in accounting. Purple-haired lady in marketing who seems cool, but I forget her name. British lady who brings the good tea for the break room and is either named Louise or Hermione. I should probably go around and introduce myself to everyone one of these days. I like it here.

And there she is. The woman who saved Christmas. The woman who handles me with the sleek, unruffled grace of a manga geisha drawn by a total pervert. She's wearing that same fucking outfit she wore when she traveled to Cleveland. The sweater dress. The boots. Different black see-through tights, obviously, because I ripped the other ones to shreds. She's got the same welcoming *I dare you to mess with me right now* smirk on her face that she's greeted me with ever since I hired her.

She's standing by her desk with a coffee mug in one hand, her other hand resting just above her hip, right where I was gripping her on my kitchen counter earlier. This is working for me. We can do this.

"Morning, Cooper."

"Good morning, Mr. Cannavale." She hands me the ***World's Best Boss*** mug. It's strong and black, just the way I like it.

"Nice orchids."

"Thanks. A very thoughtful asshole gave them to me." She follows me into my office and leaves the door open. "I printed out your call sheet, and I've already replied to a few emails that you don't have to deal with."

I fucking love you is what I want to say. "Thanks. Did you see that Drucker actually closed a deal in the Hamptons yesterday? I'll have to talk to him later." I wait for her to tell me he's already on my call sheet or that she's already responded to his stupid email question for me. But she doesn't.

When I glance up at her, she isn't smirking and she isn't smiling. She isn't staring at me with heavy-lidded eyes and heaving breasts. She isn't even frowning at me in that way that makes me want to tug on her hair and really give her something to frown about. She isn't doing any of the things I like to see her do in response to me. She's frowning at me in an entirely new way that I don't like at all. I know that frown. I've seen that frown on another woman's face, and the words that come out of that frowny mouth next are never good.

"You okay?"

It takes her a moment, but she snaps out of her unpleasant musing and answers, "Yeah. Let me know when you're ready to roll calls. I'm just going through the Hamptons contract for you right now." And with that, she leaves my office and shuts the door. One second later, she opens the door again. "Sorry, did you want this open or closed?"

"Open."

"Right." She goes back to her desk and doesn't look over at me once she sits down.

Which is probably fine.

Either that or it's terrible.

I mean, I did tell her we wouldn't be discussing our extracurricular activities at the office.

And I don't have time to wonder what's up, because of the shit-ton of calls and emails and the half a shit-ton of contracts I have to go over before we leave for Cleveland. Maddie knows this better than anyone. Which is why she's leaving me alone to let me work instead of getting into a discussion about her feelings. Which is why she's the best assistant I've ever had. Which is why I don't want to lose her.

After a few hours of powering through the most urgent calls and emails and skimming through a few contracts, I get up to stretch my legs. Standing just inside my doorway, I wait for Maddie to look up from her computer monitor. She doesn't seem to be typing or reading. She's just staring ahead.

"Should we order lunch?" I ask, startling her.

She contemplates this for an excruciatingly long time, like I've asked her if she ever wants to eat lunch again for the rest of her life. "Hang on," she finally says. She stands up and rounds her desk, heading toward me. She gestures for me to step aside, walks into my office, and shuts the door.

"Well now. I wasn't talking about ordering *that* kind of lunch, but let me close the blinds…"

She sighs, a long, sad sigh.

"Dec. I've been thinking about this a lot for the past couple of days, and I don't know if this is a good idea."

"What do you mean?"

"You know what I mean. I don't think I can do this anymore."

And there it is. The other shoe.

Most days, I'm beyond grateful to have the mind of a legal professional. Most of the time it keeps me out of trouble because I'm always thinking ahead, looking at things from every possible angle. I wish I could say that I didn't see this coming, and I wish I could say that I hadn't planned a response for it. But I did, and I have.

Here we go…

THIRTY-ONE

Maddie

YOUR NUTS ROASTING ON AN OPEN FIRE

Declan studies my face for about a year, and I can't for the life of me read his expression.

Fucking lawyers.

I'm finally ready to have an actual discussion about my real feelings and what I want, but I can see the wheels turning in his head. He's going to present his closing arguments to the jury. I'm about to get run over by the attorney train.

He crosses his arms in front of his chest and says, "Yeah, I know. Too good to be true, right? Just a matter of time before things get complicated."

"Declan…I just can't—"

He cuts me off and starts pacing back and forth. "No, I get it, you're right. Let's stay ahead of this. The whole point of that document was to ensure that we don't let this interfere with our work and our dynamic here at Sentinel."

"Exactly."

"Exactly. So as long as you aren't planning to sue me for sexual harassment, then we're good."

I scoff and roll my eyes, shaking my head. The usual response to his baloney general counsel personality, but Jesus that stings. "Is that really all you're worried about right now?"

"I'd like a verbal reaffirmation that you won't be taking this up with HR, Maddie."

"I won't be taking it up with HR, Declan. But I *would* like to shove that document up your—"

"Don't worry, I won't force you to come to the office while I'm attending the rest of my family events alone. So you'll have nothing to complain about."

"Hah! Beg to differ."

His eyes, usually an intoxicating warm shade of whiskey brown, are now iced black coffee. The kind that give you a headache and diarrhea. The kind that you eagerly consume for a sudden burst of energy and then causes you to question all of your life choices when you crash and burn. I can't look at him.

Declan Cannavale has always made my blood boil for a variety of reasons, but now that there's love in my heart, I don't know if it can handle this. Apparently the secret to being his assistant and dealing with his bullshit was believing that there was nothing to him besides the bullshit. Even now, all I see is the guy who sat on my aunt's sofa watching a romantic comedy with my dad. I don't think I can stand Office Declan anymore.

"I'll just go to Cleveland by myself tomorrow,

then. Do you have any requests as to what kind of lie I should tell my family regarding the reason for your absence? Fear of flying? Food poisoning? Or should I just tell them we broke up?"

I whip around to face him again. "For your information, I wasn't talking about not going with you to Cleveland. I was trying to tell you that I don't think I can work for you anymore."

He had this same look on his face after I slapped him in that hotel elevator. "You're joking, right?"

"Why would I joke about that?"

"You want to quit being my assistant?"

"Well, I wouldn't be the first to do that now, would I?"

"Some of them were fired. Most of them were fired. Because none of them were as good as you. You can't quit. We said going into this that we wouldn't let it affect our working relationship."

"You honestly don't think it has?"

"No, I don't. I got half a shit-ton of work done this morning. We're both being professionals here. We've both remained fully clothed. What's the problem?"

"The problem, Mr. Cannavale, is that I am neither a sex robot nor am I an administrative robot. I can't turn my feelings on and off like you can, and I don't want to try to do that every single day."

He keeps shaking his head, like I'm speaking a foreign language. "So let me get this straight… You're talking about—what? Quitting the job but continuing to pretend to be my girlfriend until after my brother's wedding?"

And there it is.

The word *pretend.*

That's all it is to him.

I can't believe it didn't even occur to me that he was just pretending all this time.

There's a steaming hot lump of something in my throat. I want to burst into tears and scream *Liar liar, I'm going to set your pants on fire!* But I'm going to summon up all of my inner strength and channel Julianna Margulies from every episode I've ever seen of *The Good Wife* instead. Take the high road. Get off the emotional roller coaster. Make a rational decision and then calmly express it and leave. "Actually, I don't want to go to Cleveland with you anymore either, Declan. I quit all of it."

He clenches his jaw, but there's that flash of something in his iced coffee eyes that reminds me of the warmth in him.

I look away again because if I don't take the heat that's rising in me and use it to roast his nuts on an open fire, then we'll just have sex on the floor of his office, and I'll still end up with the same problem.

I not only fell for my boss, but I fell for an act.

Or some alcohol and carb-induced holiday reverie. A rated-R version of *The Nutcracker*. The nutcracker that turned into a naked dancing prince was just a dream. Now I'm waking up to a rat in a suit.

"You're just going to leave me?" His voice is cold and flat.

"I'm giving you my two weeks' notice. I'll find and train my replacement."

"You're doing the exact thing I told you I don't want you to do."

"I'm not filing a claim with HR, Declan. I just can't work for you anymore, and I can't believe you don't understand why."

"I need you here as my assistant. What do you want—a raise?"

"Go to hell, Declan."

"Yeah, because *I'm* the asshole—it's never the one who walks away."

I almost make it to the door. I almost manage to bite my tongue and keep my mouth shut. But I spin around to face him and say, "You know what I think? I think Hannah probably walked away after years of trying to get through to you. But you never heard a word she said because you were so busy trying to convince her you were right that you couldn't even see what was wrong. And I'm not saying there's anything wrong with who you are or who you and I were together these past few days. I loved the time we spent together. You'll never know how much. But I'm not going to spend one more second pretending that I'm okay with this." I put my hand on the door handle and wait for him to say something, anything.

But he doesn't.

I glance back at him, and it is chilling, the way he's looking at me. I either hit a nerve or an artery, and he clearly didn't hear a word that I said after the Hannah thing. He has no rebuttal. And he clearly does not want me to continue talking.

So I open the door.

"If you leave now, don't bother coming back," he mutters.

"Fine. Don't bother calling or texting me, because I won't respond. It's not my job to anymore."

"Oh, and don't worry—I'll still give you a good letter of recommendation if you need one. About your administrative skills, I mean. Not as a fake girlfriend."

I have no idea what Julianna Margulies would say in this situation on *The Good Wife*, but I let my middle finger do the talking for me.

I don't slam the door shut, because there are at least five other people here today and also because there are dampers on all of the office doors to prevent them from slamming shut. But I have never wanted to slam a door so badly in my life. Or to throw a desk through a glass wall—or a lawyer.

Or to punch something.

At least I can go home and do that, thanks to the thoughtful asshole who gave me a punching bag for Christmas.

Merry fucking December 28th to me.

Chapter Thirty-Two

MADDIE: Hi. <sad face emoji>
DECLAN: Hi Piper.
MADDIE: Yeah. It's me. I'll delete this convo from her phone when we're done. She's here talking to my mom in the other room. Rough day, huh?
DECLAN: It's not great. She okay?
MADDIE: I've never seen her this smad before, TBH.
DECLAN: I don't know what TBH means. Or smad.
MADDIE: TBH=to be honest. Smad=sad and mad.
DECLAN: Ahh. I tried calling and texting her and going to her place after she left, but she won't respond. I don't blame her. I was a total asshole.
MADDIE: IMO she just needs time. IMO=in my opinion FYI. FYI=for your info.

DECLAN: LOL I do know what IMO and FYI stand for, thanks.
MADDIE: Oh cool.
DECLAN: I never wanted things to end up like this.
MADDIE: Neither did she. But it's not my place to speak for her. Hey, so if you need someone else to go to the wedding with you and pretend to be your GF, I am available!!! LOLOL.
DECLAN: You're a great kid, Piper. One day, some guy will be lucky to have you. When you're twenty-five or so.
MADDIE: Maybe by then I'll have boobs.
DECLAN: I cannot comfortably respond to that, sorry. But you're great no matter what.
MADDIE: Well anyway. Maybe you should try her again tomorrow. Give her some time to cool down. Give yourself some time to cool down too?
DECLAN: You're very wise. Except I have to go to Cleveland to be with my brother tomorrow morning. But I'll try calling or texting.
MADDIE: Okay. And also, if Eddie needs a date let him know that I'm available too LOLOL JK but not really.
DECLAN: You got it. Take care. Don't forget to delete this conversation.
MADDIE: I'll do it now. See you later. I hope.

DECLAN: I hope so too. Have a happy new year.
MADDIE: <red heart emoji>

THIRTY-THREE

Declan

THE WORST MAN HOLIDAY

Everything in this suite at the Cleveland Ritz-Carlton is mocking me. The king-size bed that Maddie won't be in when I return tonight. The view that I can't look out at with her. The orchids that I know she'd love. I could be pleasuring Maddie Cooper under the rainforest shower head right now. Instead, I'm Googling *"what to eat before drinking alcohol"* and trying to order bananas, salmon, eggs, sweet potatoes, and hummus from in-room dining before Billy Boston and Irish Nolan show up to kidnap me.

"I have no idea what Korean pear juice tastes like," I tell the moron on the other end of the line. It's not his fault that I didn't feel like eating on the plane. However, it is definitely his fault that the kitchen doesn't stock Korean pear juice. "But I'm pretty sure that apple juice is not a comparable substitute. If drinking apple juice could prevent a hangover, then

I'm pretty sure they'd just say that in the article, Raymond. Let me speak to your supervisor—you know what, never mind. I don't want any of it. Cancel my order. This is horse shit." I hang up the hotel phone, cursing Raymond, my life, the world, tomorrow's inevitable hangover, and every single thing I said to Maddie in my office yesterday.

I don't know why it hadn't even occurred to me that she'd want to quit for any reason other than hating my guts. So as soon as she brought it up, my brain just shut down. I was already in defense-mode, but all I could do was think about how shitty my life would be if she weren't my assistant anymore. I didn't even have time to think about what it would be like if she isn't in it the way she had been since the 23rd. For a guy who prides himself on saying all the right things at the right time, I totally shit the bed.

All I needed to do was listen to what she was saying and tell her how I felt, but I didn't.

I threw myself into work for a couple of hours after she left, because that's what I do. But once I'd blasted through everything, and the dust settled, I finally heard what she'd said. I finally heard what I'd actually said and realized five important things. One: I suck at relationships. Two: What she said about Hannah and me stung because she was right. Three: I can't function without Maddie in my life. Four: I will do whatever it takes to let Maddie know how much she means to me. Five: I also have an obligation to my brother and my entire family to be here for this wedding, and the timing sucks almost as much as I do.

I can damage control almost any corporate nightmare that any idiot can throw my way, but apparently I'm still a novice at cleaning up my own messes. None of this is news to me—I knew I'd fuck things up with Maddie eventually. I just didn't expect it to happen so soon. I honestly didn't expect to fall for her as hard as I did. And I certainly didn't expect her to feel anything other than lust for me either.

I reach for my cell phone, which has been charging ever since I got to the room. I can't believe I'm taking advice from a thirteen-year-old girl, but Piper probably knows more about Maddie than I do. I intend to change that of course, but hopefully she was right about Maddie only needing a day or so to cool down.

Just as I'm opening up my phone app, I get a call from my sister.

"Hey, Case. Can I call you right back?"

"No. What kind of asshole answers the phone like that? You at the hotel?"

"Yes. What kind of asshat won't let someone call them back?"

"You know what—I wasn't even calling for you. I need to talk to Maddie."

"Why?"

"We forgot to invite her to our spa day while you guys are out stirring up trouble. And by the way—keep your eye on my husband. If he gets anywhere near another woman today, I will castrate all of you."

"That's a pretty picture. I don't think you have anything to worry about—have you not seen Aiden's itinerary? The first stop on the party bus ride from hell is a Dave & Buster's."

"Yeah, you know how much respect Billy and Nolan have for Aiden's itinerary? About as much respect as they have for your liver. Good luck not puking your brains out. Put Maddie on."

What to say, what to say, what to say…

"Maddie isn't here, actually…yet."

Fuck you, optimism.

"What do you mean?"

"She had a minor family emergency to attend to, but she'll try to make it to the wedding. Probably. We'll see."

"Dec…"

"What? What am I supposed to do—not let her deal with a minor family emergency?"

The emergency being that she has to tell her family how big of an asshole I am.

"She's not coming?"

"I didn't say that. I just said she isn't here. Look, I have to call her before the guys get here. Have a great spa day—I promise to keep your husband in line. See you tomorrow." I hang up. I never hang up on my sister before she's said goodbye first. I'm in a downward spiral.

I start typing out a text to Maddie. It seems like the smart thing to do—take her temperature first before calling—since I'm not exactly bringing my A-game with the ladies today. Before I've even finished typing three sentences, my mother calls.

And I know, even before I answer, exactly how this conversation is going to go.

"Hey, Ma."

"Dec. Why isn't Maddie here? What happened?"

"It's just what I told Casey." I say a quick prayer, just in case there's a chance she's so busy she'll actually fall for that crap.

"Don't you give me that, mister. There's something wrong. I can hear it in your voice. You're hungry and you're anxious. Tell me. Or, you know... If you'd feel better lying to your only sister *and* your only mother, then just keep doing that. Go on. I've got a million relatives coming into town and a house to clean, but I got all the time in the world over here."

"We had an argument, okay? She quit."

"She quit her job?"

"Yes. And she quit...being my fake girlfriend."

"What did you just say? She quit being your *fake* girlfriend? Did my sixty-year-old ears hear that right?"

"Yes. I know it sounds weird—"

"Ya think?"

"But that's just how it started out. Things got real, fast. And they were good. They were better than good. They were better than anything. And then I messed up, but I'll make it right. I just have to talk to her before the guys get here."

I can hear her sniffling, which is awesome.

"Ma. Don't cry."

Well, this is a fucking delightful unexpected treat.

"Aw, Decky, I'm sorry. I'm sorry you felt so bad

about everything that you had to go and fake a girlfriend."

"It's no one's fault, Ma. Well, maybe it's my fault."

"I like her, Dec. I like Maddie. I like her with you. Even Nonna likes her."

"I know. I do too."

"I just don't know where I went wrong with you. You were such a good boy. Always my little angel—I don't know why you can't get it right with a girl."

"I wish I knew. I thought I was doing pretty good, too… You think I should go back to New York real quick to fix this?"

"Declan Sullivan Cannavale, don't you dare! You can't leave your brother with those animals—Aiden and Eddie can't handle them."

"Those animals from *your* side of the family, you mean?"

"You should be Brady's best man—we don't talk about it, but you know it."

"Yeah. I know."

"Least you could do is be there for him for the next few days."

"Yes. Least I could do after providing him with a bride."

"All right, that's enough about that."

There's banging on the door.

"Eh! Room service! Somebody in there order a wicked awesome steamin' pile of trouble?!"

"Shut your feckin' gob, O'Sullivan—this here's a fine establishment."

"Shit," I whisper into the phone. "They're here. I gotta go."

"Me too. I gotta pick your granny and grandad up at the airport."

"Oh good. His foot's better?"

"Enh. Good enough. Love you, Dec. Don't screw up your life. But don't let those boys screw up Brady's wedding for him either. And I don't want all you boys showing up for the rehearsal all banjaxed and unshowered!"

"On it. I'll take care of all of it. Love you too. Bye."

I check the text that I had started writing to Maddie and delete it without sending. I'll try again when we're in the party limo. I roll my eyes and gird my loins, because what the fuck are a bunch of grown men doing getting into a party limo at one in the afternoon anyway?

More banging on the door. "You in there, Dec?" It's Brady, and he sounds mildly frightened.

"Yeah. Coming." I grab my coat, slide my phone into an inside pocket.

As soon as I unlock the door, Billy O'Sullivan comes bursting through it. He gets me in a headlock and shouts out, "Eh, Manhattan! Look at this ugly mug. I missed this mug so hard all these years." Billy has burst through every door he's ever walked through, and he shouts in his sleep. I'm already exhausted. He looks around at the suite and lets go of me. "Whoa. Check out this wicked fuckin' pissa hotel room!"

"Should we get going?" I ask as he bounds over to the windows.

My Irish cousin Nolan squeezes my shoulder and hands me a can of Guinness in a brown paper bag as he passes by while unzipping his jeans. "Drink up, cousin. I need to hit the jacks."

I do appreciate that the can is unopened, because the last time I drank from an open container that he presented to me, here is what I've pieced together about how the next 48 hours played out: Nolan shaved the front part of my legs. We all ended up on stage at a Steve Miller Band concert singing "The Joker." We took over the drive-thru window at a Taco Bell. I sang that Chumbawamba song into the mic and bought tacos for everyone who came through—with my new credit card. The next morning, I tried to adopt all of the dogs at an animal shelter in Toledo and cried for half an hour when they wouldn't let me. No one really knows how we ended up in Michigan.

I pull my brother in for a hug. "Having fun yet?"

"I can't wait to never go out without my wife again. Or just to never go out again."

"Sounds good." *Sounds really good. I am not going to cry.*

"Sorry, is it weird for you when I call your ex-girlfriend my wife?" he asks with a smirk.

"Naw. Is it weird for *you* when she screams my name out during sex?"

"Oooh, touché."

Touché. Brady is the only person in my entire

family who would ever use that word, and I love him for it.

I catch Billy pulling snacks out of the minibar. "Hey. Don't touch those."

"Aww, come on. I'm starvin'!"

"There's supposed to be food in the party bus—I Venmo'd Aiden money for it."

"Naw, we spent it on *lickah* instead. Tell you what—you finish that can of Guinness before we leave this room, and I won't touch your mini bar."

"Fuck off. You can pick one snack." I hold up a finger for emphasis, like I'm talking to a child. "*One*."

Brady lowers his voice and says, "So, Casey just texted me that Maddie isn't coming, and she was just pretending to be your girlfriend? What's going on? Are you okay?"

"Yeah, I'm okay. Don't even worry about me—this is your day to relax and have fun."

"You sure? If you want to talk about it…"

I'm actually dying to talk about it. It is literally the only thing I want to talk about all of a sudden, because it's all I want to think about. But my brother looks so concerned, and it's his bachelor party day, and I'm not *that* self-absorbed and miserable. Yet.

I crack open the can of Guinness. "I'm sure." I raise the can to him. "May the best day of your past be the worst day of your future."

After guzzling about half of it, I let him take it from me so he can toast me with: "May your heart be light and happy, may your smile be big and wide. May we survive this feckin' shit so that I can claim my bride."

After both of my cousins have finally finished polluting my luxury bathroom, I'm a little buzzed and stepping inside the luxury party bus that is basically a cheesy bachelor pad on wheels. It is in no way as funny to me as the cheesy stretch limo that Maddie got for us, because my older brother did not order it ironically.

Around the navy blue leather perimeter seating are my oldest brother Aiden, youngest brother Eddie, Casey's husband, Billy's married brother Mark, and the married Irish cousins, Sean and Fergal. Everyone else is dressed more casually than I am, as usual. I greet everyone, and Nolan places another unopened can of Guinness in all of our hands.

"To the brewery and then the casino!" Billy yells out after chatting with the driver.

"I thought we're going to Dave & Buster's first," I say, looking at Aiden and Brady.

Aiden stares down at the floor meekly and takes a sip of beer.

"Nawww! Fuck that kiddie shit—what are we, twelve? Change of plans. We're havin' some actual fun instead. Drink up, Manhattan."

This is bullshit.

I nudge Brady, who's sitting beside me and texting Hannah. "You okay with this?"

He shrugs. "Doesn't really matter where we go.

We're all going to end up hammered and facedown in the gutter by about five o'clock at this rate. Maybe if we pass out early, we'll wake up tomorrow sooner."

I muss up his hair. "Such an optimist." I pull out my phone and open up the text app.

Eddie plops down beside me. "Hey. I hear Maddie was just a fake girlfriend. Can I have her number?"

"I will actually murder you if you try anything," I mutter without even looking at him.

"I'm kidding—obviously. I have a girlfriend."

"Yeah. You meet her in person yet?"

"No, she goes to St. Bart's for New Year's every year with her friends. That's why she couldn't make it to the wedding."

"Uh-huh. And was your friend Birdie also not available to be your date?"

He laughs. "She would never go as my date to anything in a billion years. That's hilarious."

"Sucks to be you, huh?"

I finally type out the text to Maddie, impressed with how concise and eloquent I am, even after about fourteen ounces of dry stout. I hit Send as soon as I feel Nolan's Black Irish eyes on me from the back of the bus and put the phone back in my pocket.

I'm not scared of that fucker, but ever since I was a kid, I've felt the need to impress that guy. And every Irish guy, for that matter. I would laugh in Colin Firth's face if I ever meet him, but if I cross paths with Colin Farrell, I'd probably burst into tears, start quoting *In Bruges,* and try to make out with him or something.

Billy switches the Top 40 radio music to a hip hop station and cranks up the volume before shaking up a bottle of champagne and popping the cork, spraying bubbly everywhere like an asshole.

I don't even finish the whole can of Guinness before Nolan silently exchanges it for another full one. I know this trick. It's harder to keep track of how much I've had this way. Not falling for it. Not this time.

I type out another text to Maddie because I remember something really important that I wanted to tell her, and then hit Send before Billy comes over to hassle all four of us brothers for texting our women when we should be partying.

"Whatta *yiz* doin' *ovah heah*? This a *bachelah pawty* or a fuckin' pussy convention?"

I send Maddie one more impassioned text before slipping my phone back into my coat pocket as Nolan sits down between me and Brady, flicking at his scruffy face and staring me down like an Irish gangster.

"You're here to have fun, are you not?" he calmly asks.

"To a degree," I say. Holding my ground. "We're gonna pace ourselves. I promised my ma and my sister I'd keep my brothers out of trouble. You wouldn't want to upset my ma and my sister now, would you?"

He grins and pulls a flask out of the pocket of his leather jacket. "You wouldn't want to disappoint your Irish ancestors, now would you?"

Some sober voice in my head starts reciting every

single thing I should be saying on the phone to Maddie right now, but I can't quite hear it over the din of my drunk Irish ancestors taunting me.

"Forgive me, Cooper," I whisper into the flask as I slowly bring it to my lips.

THIRTY-FOUR

Maddie

SHOULD OLD ASSISTANTS BE FORGOT

Well, I gotta hand it to Declan—no one has ever given me a more useful Christmas present in my life. I only allowed myself one glass of wine at my sister's place yesterday because I didn't want to risk getting all maudlin and drunk-texting him after so emphatically telling him not to text me when I left the office. But instead of waking up with a hangover this morning, I have bruised fists.

Worth it. I got out a lot of aggression with that punching bag. But I had to remove the picture of him that I'd taped to it, because it just made me sad, and I didn't even want to pretend to mess up that annoyingly handsome face.

First he's got me overworking my erotic massage tool, and now I'm abusing the punching bag.

Okay, I may have also abused the erotic massage tool last night. And again this morning. Because not having a job is stressful. I emailed a headhunter shortly after I got up, to let her know that I'm looking for a new position, and she called me back immediately to discuss my options. She didn't even ask why I was leaving my current position—I suppose because she has already found jobs for numerous other former executive assistants who have had the misfortune of working for Declan Cannavale.

I went out to run some errands when I knew Mrs. Pavlovsky would be in her apartment eating lunch, because I didn't want to risk seeing her disappointed face. Declan had come by the building yesterday, and I wouldn't let him in. She came by my door to ask if she could let him in. When I asked her not to, she was only slightly less dramatic than the heroine of every film I've ever seen that's based on a Russian novel. Now that I've returned and put the groceries away, I casually check my phone to see if the recruiter *or anyone else* has contacted me.

There are a bunch of texts from Declan and a couple of voice mail messages, and I am so mad at my stupid heart for racing as soon as I see the notifications. I'm so furious with my idiot stomach butterflies for taking flight as I open up the texts.

DECLAN: Hi. I know you said not to bother texting you, and even though you are the boss of me, I have never been good at letting someone else have the last word. There is one

thing and one thing only that I should have said to you yesterday, Maddie... I

That's it. He just wrote "I." Like that's what he should have said to me yesterday. As if every single thing he said wasn't about him.

DECLAN: Also, what you said about me and hands was right. I don't want to be like that anymore. You deserve better.

I mean. I think he may have meant "me and Hannah," but it's the "You deserve better" part that concerns me, since that has historically been code for "I've met someone else, so let's take a break and start seeing other people." The time stamp for the next text is about half an hour later.

DECLAN: Cooper. I miss you all. I done know if I deserve forgive but please give me another change. I'll do anyway.

I want to laugh because he's obviously drunk, but I also wouldn't put it past him to ask me to change for him. Or maybe he wants me to loan him some quarters.

Then I listen to the voice mails. The first one is just Declan singing the first half of "My Heart Will Go On" into the phone before getting cut off. I can hear a bunch of grown men yelling the words to a Beastie Boys song in the background. It's an aural fustercluck.

The next message is probably a pocket dial. At least I hope it is. I can hear a bunch of guys singing the Meatloaf song "I'd Do Anything for Love," and Declan is singing the girl's part.

After listening to those messages again, I find another text notification.

DECLAN: Copppperrrrr. Please done be Maddie at me. I never fell like thish around anyone before. I ducked up. I wished yo were here. I ned young. Brb <kissing face emoji> <crying face emoji> <nail polish emoji>

Before I can even try to decipher what the hell he meant by this message, I receive another one.

DECLAN: Right. Howya, gorgeous. Time for Dec to put the phone away and join his family now. Happy New Year to ya.

. . .

So that's that. Not that I would have responded. Because what am I supposed to say to any of that? I just hope that dumbass remembered to eat before he started drinking, because he sounded hungry to me.

I listen to the voice mails one more time before putting my phone in my purse and leaving for Sentinel with a storage box. At least I know I won't run into Declan when I collect my things from my desk. I do, however, run into Mrs. Pavlovsky when I'm walking out to my car.

She looks exactly as heartbroken as I had feared she would when she sees me. It's freezing out, but at least she's wearing a brand-new wool coat while sweeping the very clean sidewalk in front of our building.

"Oh, you got a new coat!"

She tears up as she strokes the collar. "Yes. Beautiful kind man bring me yesterday."

"Declan gave you a coat?"

She nods and sighs. "He seem very upset. But you also seem upset, so I did not let him in. But I *vanted* to, Magdalena. Ohhh, I *vanted* to. It was very hard."

"I know. I'm sorry." I rub her arm. "Thank you for respecting my wishes. And don't forget to work on your *w* sounds."

She pouts and then licks her lips and says, "I wish you will be happy with him."

Cindy is singing "Don't Stop Believin'" into her karaoke machine at the reception desk when I arrive at Sentinal.

She pauses the music as soon as she sees me, but it's not because she's embarrassed to be caught singing. She's staring at my storage box and looking very concerned.

"Hi," she says. "Are you leaving us?"

"Yeah. Don't stop singing, though. You sounded great."

She completely disregards my compliment. "Oh no—Maddie. Why?"

"Oh, you know. This job just isn't a good fit for me."

"Did he fire you?"

"No. It was my idea."

"Oh. Did things get…complicated?"

I look around to see if anyone is within earshot.

"No one else is here," she assures me. "Otherwise I wouldn't be singing… Did things get weird after McSorley's?"

"No, not at all!" I did not mean to yell that. "It's just time for me to move on."

She twists her lips to one side. "After two months?"

I look away because there isn't much else that I can say.

"Well, I won't keep you, but I'll miss you. Stay in touch, okay?"

"I will, definitely."

As I'm walking away, she says, "You know, he went through seven other assistants here before he hired you."

"I'm well aware of that, yeah. He's pretty demanding."

"Yeah, but I mean…you're the only one he actually made stay late with him."

"I am?"

"He'd always send the others home early because it was easier for him to do everything himself, he said."

"Oh." I stare down at the empty box in my hands. "I didn't know that."

Fuck you, nose tingles.

"I didn't even know the poor guy could smile until two months ago."

Not now, tear ducts!

"Yeah, well…hopefully his next assistant will be even better for him," I manage to say through the lump in my throat. "Oh, and Cindy… Don't tell him I told you this, but Declan was your Secret Santa."

Her eyes widen, her lower lip quivers, and now there are three women in Manhattan that I know of who are all teary-eyed over that asshole.

When I'm almost done packing up my personal items, I get a call on my cell phone. It's my former boss, Artie. Maybe he's finally going to do me a solid and come out of retirement so I can work for him again. "Hello? Artie?"

"Happy holidays, honey."

It warms my heart to hear his voice. "Happy holidays! Is everything okay?"

"Well, that's what I was calling to ask *you*, Maddie. I just got off the phone with a recruiter. She was confirming that she could use my recommendation letter for you. Don't tell me you're leaving Declan already."

I clear my throat and try to sound as chipper as possible. "Just needed something new for the New Year," I say totally unconvincingly.

He sighs. "You don't have to tell me. I'll support you, no matter what." We're both silent for a long beat before he continues. "I just wanted to tell you something. Something that I had forgotten until recently. Since you won't be working for him anymore…"

I blow out a laugh. "You finally going to warn me about Declan Cannavale's moods? You're a little late."

"I told you, I don't know anything about that," he says jovially. "You remember that time I had lunch with him? When you were still working for me, and he was still at the law firm? He'd asked me to consult on something, and I forgot to bring some papers with me. You swung by the restaurant to drop them off."

"I do remember that." That was back when Declan and I used to chat on the phone whenever he'd call for Artie, and I thought it was odd that he'd started making those calls himself.

"I met you outside, but I guess Declan could see you from inside the restaurant. He was always telling me over the phone that I was lucky to have an assistant who was so on the ball. But when I went back inside and sat down, he told me to let him know as soon as I was planning to retire because he wanted to hire you. This would have been a year before you ended up working for him."

"Oh" is all I can say as I stroke the petals of an orchid bloom and stare at the empty desk through the glass wall opposite me.

"I think he was living with someone back then. But he seemed a little distracted for the rest of lunch. I think he's had a thing for you for quite some time."

I snort-laugh at that. "I don't think so."

"Well, I don't know the story, but speaking as a former boss who had a crush on his assistant…"

I cringe for a terrible second.

"Not you, honey—my wife! Did I not tell you that she was my assistant before we married? Things were a little less complicated back then, of course. But it's never easy to navigate that kind of situation. I'm not saying you should keep working for him. Maybe it's best if you don't. It's none of my business, but you've always been like a daughter to me. I'm just saying, in case things got complicated between the two of you… Maybe see what it's like when you aren't working together. After all those other boyfriends I've seen you with over the years—you deserve a guy like him."

"Wow. He seems to have developed himself quite a fanbase outside of his former assistants."

"I'm saying this because I'm a fan of *you*, Maddie. I know we lawyers aren't the easiest people to work with or live with. But some people are better suited to working and living with us than others." He chuckles. I always loved it when he'd chuckle like that. Like Santa Claus. "Like it or not, you're one of the people who can actually handle us. Doesn't mean you *have* to deal with a lawyer personally and professionally. But if you are looking for something new for next year, maybe you and Declan can both start over with a clean slate… Said my piece. And as I told the recruiter, I'll sing your praises to whoever will listen."

I thank Artie, tell him to say "hi" to the missus for me, and hang up. When I look at the texts that Declan had sent earlier, I try re-reading them with a slightly less cynical perspective. And all of a sudden, I can fill in the blanks and rearrange all of the sentences that matter: *I love you. I miss you already. Please give me another chance. I'll do anything. Please don't be mad at me. I've never felt like this about anyone before. I fucked up. I wish you were here. I need you.*

I have no idea what the nail polish emoji was all about, but I think I know what Declan Cannavale is all about now.

And *I never fell like thish around anyone before* either.

I hope we haven't ducked things up completely.

THIRTY-FIVE

Piper

THE BUTTSMACKER

December 30th

Dear Diary,

Today Mom, Aunt Maddie and I basically acted out the climax of every romantic comedy I have ever seen, and one that I plan to write one day when my parents finally give me the screenwriting software I've been asking for since I was twelve.

Let's just say that if there is such a thing as romantic karma, then my boobs are going to get really big, and my first boyfriend will have the best butt in school (although not necessarily **my** ***school because my New Year's resolution is to expand my horizons and also crush on boys from other schools).***

Anyway. Aunt Maddie wasn't sure if she should go to Cleveland to be with Declan since

he wasn't answering his phone and hadn't responded to her text messages. Mom and I were like—OMG you have to go! How can you not go?! You have to go to him and tell him you love him and HEA with him because #Maclan! Like what is she even thinking? He has the best butt in all the land. Well, I mean it's tied with his brother Eddie's although I've never seen his IRL. They may use a stunt butt on the show IDK.

So Dad watched the baby and Mom and I drove over to Maddie's. While my mom was still driving around trying to find parking and my aunt was busy finding a flight, I packed a suitcase for her. I packed up all the outfits that I would wear for Declan if I could. She'll thank me later. Or more like Declan will!

She got a ticket for a flight that was leaving in two and a half hours, so we had to book it!

We rushed to the airport and Mom's driving wasn't nearly as slow and annoying as usual since the baby wasn't in the car with us. Aunt Maddie was more nervous than I've ever seen her, so Mom gave her a tiny bottle of something called Bailey's that she said her Aunt Mel put in her purse "to help get her through the holidays." And then she put on that Cranberries song "Dreams," and we all sang it at the top of our lungs.

When we pulled up to drop Maddie off, my

mom said the best thing she's ever said, and I'm so proud of her.

She said: "I know I'm the older sister, but you've always been the big sis in this family. You're always the one to help get everyone else's shit together, including mine. Declan might be drunk off his ass right now, and he might need you, but probably not in the way that it seemed when you were his assistant. No guy would show up at a family dinner on Staten Island unless he needed the woman he was showing up for in his life all the time. But some guys need a big old smack on the butt to get them to realize it's time for them to man up. Now it's time for you to let that man know you're his woman. Smack that butt, girl. And bring that butt home for all of us because OMG it's perfect."

Okay, I may have rewritten your little monologue a tiny bit, but that was basically what you said. That's right, Mom. I know you read my diary and I don't mind you knowing this: it was really cool that you said that. It was super exciting to be a part of #Maclan's HEA and it was basically the most fun we've had together all year. I guess I've missed hanging out with you.

Hopefully Aunt Maddie will get there in time for the rehearsal dinner.

But seriously—you have to stop reading my diary.

THIRTY-SIX

Declan

TRY HARD. TRY HARDER. TRY HARD WITH A VENGEANCE.

Everything is terrible, and I'm an idiot.

When I wake up, I am fully dressed in the bathtub of my hotel suite.

That's the good news—that I wake up and that I'm in my hotel suite in Cleveland.

The other news is I'm wearing Nolan's clothes, which are a couple of sizes too big for me, and a bachelorette party novelty trucker hat. I carefully remove it from my head and see that it says ***Shot Queen.*** Which makes sense. My brain has been replaced with a pulsating lead boulder, I'm pretty sure I got run over by an SUV at some point, and it feels like somebody put a cigar out on my tongue. Ghosts are trying to pull my hair follicles out one by one, and I think I see those twin girls from *The Shining* over by the toilet.

My Irish ancestors clearly hate me.

Everything hurts, including my heart, and the first thought that emerges from the quicksand of my mind is, *"Maddie. I have to call Maddie."*

The desire to see Maddie and hear her voice again is the only thing stronger than my desire to sleep for another week or two. As long as she doesn't yell at me. And as long as I don't have to keep my eyelids open for more than a second at a time. Or lift my head up.

I promise myself that if I am, in fact, alive—and I'm not entirely sure that I am yet—that I will live each day of the rest of my god-forsaken life doing whatever it takes to make things up to Maddie.

I will be the best man that anyone could be for her.

Or I will try to be the best man that I can be for her, anyway.

I will try really hard.

As soon as the nausea passes.

I feel around for my phone and find it in one of the pockets of Nolan's leather jacket, along with a bunch of condom packets and paper napkins with women's names and numbers on them. I am confident that Nolan was the one who was wearing this jacket and collecting phone numbers for most of the night, and I want to murder him because he must have had my phone on him for most of last night too.

At least I hope it was last night that we went out. It had better still be December 30th.

My phone is dead, of course. So I crawl out of the

bathtub in search of my charger and the nearest outlet that is as close to the ground as possible. Because I will be staying as close to the ground as possible for as long as possible.

The clock by the bed tells me it's 2:47 pm, but it doesn't tell me what day it is because it's an asshole.

Nolan is passed out on the floor right beside the bed, with a hat that says ***Designated Drunk.*** Surprisingly, he is not wearing my clothes. He is wearing my cousin Billy's clothes. Billy is sprawled out on the bed. It looks like he had fallen asleep while he was in the middle of either putting my clothes on or taking them off. His trucker hat says ***Dancing Diva***, and to my understated delight, someone has drawn a penis on his forehead in black ink. I hope it was me.

I pull the hotel phone down off the desk, randomly press a button, and ask whoever answers to send all the coffee to my room immediately. I also ask them to call Maddie for me, but they don't know her number, and neither do I. I ask them to call my ma, and they fail me again. That's why I have to rip the phone cord from the wall and close my eyes for just a few minutes.

When I open my eyes again, the clock says 4:01 pm. We're supposed to be at the church for the rehearsal at five. That is, if it's still *today*.

I reach for a nearby shoe and hurl it at Nolan. It hits him in the face, but he doesn't even twitch. I find another shoe, toss it in Billy's general direction. It hits the wall and drops onto his head. He sniffles, mumbles "nuh-uh," and covers his head with a pillow.

My phone has been charged and halle*fucking*lujah, it's still December 30th. And there are a couple of texts from Maddie. One from last night, and one from this morning.

MADDIE: Good evening, sunshine. I got your messages earlier. Just wanted to let you know that. I've been thinking about you a lot, and I wanted you to know that too. There's a lot that I want you to know. It's not the kind of thing I want to say in a text, though. At least not when I'm sober. So if you still want me to come to Cleveland, let me know. I know you're busy with your family, so I won't get a ticket until I hear from you. I hope you ate something. I hope your heart still goes on. <winking face emoji> Mine does.

MADDIE: Morning, sunshine. I know you're busy. I just wanted you to know that I'm still here. Still in New York, I mean. But I'm still here for you too. Which is probably the cheesiest thing I've ever said out loud, but there are a lot of cheesy things I want to say to you. Let me know if you want me to come say them in person. And don't forget to hydrate.

. . .

Oh, Maddie Cooper. I will eat. I will hydrate. I will say all the cheesy things out loud to you, but not until I let you say whatever you need to say to me and listen closely and never forget a word.

There are a couple of missed call notifications from her too, but no voice mails. I call her back, but it goes straight to voice mail. I start to leave a message, but a shoe hits me in the head, and both of my cousins are suddenly awake and yelling at me to get ready to go like they've been waiting for me to wake up for hours. Assholes.

I text Maddie two words: ***Yes. Come.*** And then I get ready to go.

I wasn't able to spend much time looking at myself in the mirror, but I *feel* like I look like that alien from the Sigourney Weaver movie. If anyone cuts me, my acid blood will burn through the floor. I don't remember ever eating anything last night, but I also don't want to eat or smell any food for a few more days. Or hear music or move or talk to people. Which is unfortunate because now we're at the rehearsal dinner in a private dining room at a supper club by the river, and I am surrounded by food and music and talking people. Some of them are children. Loud children. The loudest children in the world. I know that I usually love all of these people a lot, but they all need to shut up and sit still and leave me alone so I can curl up under this table and cry while I wait to hear back from Maddie.

I stare at the empty chair at this table, pouting like a big fucking baby. I've called her six times, and it keeps going straight to voice mail. She hasn't replied to any of my texts. She may well be mad at me for not getting back to her sooner. I have no idea. I saw the texts that I had sent her last night. I was a fucking idiot. I'm lucky she was even willing to come to Cleveland after she read that mess. I suppose I should be grateful to Nolan for taking my phone away from me when he did.

Granny and Grandad O'Sullivan are sitting next to me. Granny's wearing one of those wrap dresses, and it reminds me of the one Maddie was wearing that night at the hotel in Youngstown. It's wrong. It's so wrong that I'm thinking about all the things Maddie and I did to each other that night while my granny is telling me about my grandad's foot problems. At the same time that she's talking, Grandad is telling me about the shenanigans at his bachelor party sixty-some years ago. Or rather, the stag night. Or rather, your basic night out for a bunch of Irish guys. He's told me the story ten times, so I know exactly what to say, even though I'm picturing Maddie naked right now.

"Did you get to the church on time, Grandad?" I ask when he pauses to take a breath.

"Aye. I got me to the church on time! Banjaxed, still totally langers, and I made a right bags of the wedding! Didn't I, dear wife?"

"Ohhhh, didn't you, dear husband? Made a right bags of every day of our life together since." She waves him off while simultaneously making eyes at him as he grabs her knee under the table.

"Shall I try to do better, then?" My Grandad nudges her, grinning.

"I'd like to see you try, old man. I'd like to see you try."

So, I'm not the first and I won't be the last lad in this family to screw up and then beg forgiveness from his lady love. I'm not even half as charming as my grandad—I can only hope that Maddie is twice as forgiving as my granny is.

I look across the table and see that the skin on Billy Boston's forehead is pink and raw from when he was vigorously rubbing off the penis earlier. That sounds all kinds of wrong, but absolutely nothing is right today. Like for instance, Eddie looks like he spent yesterday at the spa with the ladies instead of drinking with us—but he was definitely drinking with us. Fucking twentysomething asshole.

Actually, something is right. Brady is over there staring at Hannah like she's the queen of the universe, and even I feel a little more alive seeing the two of them together. He looks tired but happy.

According to the fifty or so new pictures I found on my phone, he spent most of the night with a big dopey grin on his face and a "pecker veil" on his head. It looks like I spent a lot of time at the brewery having a deep discussion with a waitress. According to her nametag, her name was Bernice, and according to her white hair and wrinkles, she must have been about a hundred and twenty. I'm sure she told me some really wise things about love and life, but I have forgotten all of it. It looks like I was very happy while playing the slot machines at the casino and then got very sad and angry at the craps table.

Apparently I got my aggressions out by playing the drums on stage at some music venue around town. There is also a picture of me in the drive-thru window of a Rally's, having what looks to be a very serious conversation with a guy in a truck. I was probably giving him legal advice or something. Guess I'll never know.

One thing's for certain—despite everything, I'm glad I came. It may not be thanks to me that Brady survived the night, but he survived it. I'm here for him. We're all here for him and Hannah. People have been getting up to toast them ever since dessert was served, and Eddie is wrapping up his adorable speech, so it's probably time for me to get up on the little stage and say something too.

I take another big gulp of coffee, another big gulp of water, slowly stand up, and saunter over to the stage, clapping for Eddie and for Brady and Hannah. I don't have a fucking clue what I'm going to say, and maybe that's a good thing. Maybe I'll just sing the Chumbawamba song and then drop the mic. Or maybe I'll actually say what I'm feeling when I'm feeling it instead of playing verbal chess for once in my adult life.

I pick up the microphone, and as soon as I lock eyes with Brady, I have a flashback to last night.

"Hi," I say, and then there is a very long pause because I'm trying to remember our conversation. I can tell by the way everyone is staring at me that they're afraid I'm either going to vomit or declare my love for the bride. Neither of these things are an issue. "We had a night last night, didn't we, buddy?"

"Wicked *pissah* of a night!" Billy Boston yells out, and then he drops his head to the table with a loud thud.

"That's enough outta you, Boston," I say into the mic.

Nonna is frowning and cursing at him from another table.

"Thanks for being here, buddy," Brady says, raising his glass of water to me.

"It's good to see you back in the arms of your beautiful bride, where you belong."

I wait for the "awwwws" to subside. I wasn't even playing that one for effect, but I'll take it.

"At some point last night—and to be honest, most of the night is a blur, but—at some point…I remember sitting on the ground next to Brady. We may have been hiding from our cousins…"

Pause for laughter and for Nolan to yell out, "You can run but you can't hide, Americans!"

"But I remember asking him, because I had been wondering for a long time, how long he'd known that he was in love with Hannah…"

There's a bit of murmuring, and a hush falls over the room.

"I don't mean to bring this up in a weird way," I assure the guests. "As some or all of you may know, Hannah and I dated on and off for a very long time. And as some or all of you may know, I was not the world's greatest boyfriend. I wasn't the worst—but I wasn't the great guy she deserved. Brady told me that he'd had a crush on her ever since the first time I brought her home for Thanksgiving. That was over a decade ago. That's a long time to sustain a crush. But he said he knew he was in love with her when he found out she'd left me and moved back to Cleveland, and his first instinct was to call her and not me. He said he talked himself out of calling her right away. But for the next week, she was all he could think about. And then, seemingly out of the blue, Hannah sent him a message on Facebook. She asked him the name of the book he'd mentioned at Christmas a couple of years ago. Which, as we all know, is code for 'I want you. Do something about it.'"

Pause for murmuring and laughter.

"He did something about it. He felt guilty about it. Hannah felt guilty about it. But there was no denying how they felt about each other… I was not super chill and full of grace when I found out about this. But right now, I'm about as happy as a man can be that his brother decided to date and then marry his ex-girlfriend." I look directly at Brady. "Because you knew how rare it is to find someone that you can sustain that kind of feeling for, for over a decade.

Because you both probably had feelings for each other for over a decade. But you're such classy, considerate people that you didn't act on it until I had finally blown it with Hannah for good. Because you didn't want to waste any more time *not* being her husband.

"I get that. There's a woman I had a crush on ever since the first time I saw her too. Ever since the first time I spoke to her on the phone, to be honest. She had been all I could think about for over two months. And I know without a doubt that she will dominate my thoughts for the rest of my life. I know that I'm crazy in love with her. The problem is, I'm nothing like Brady. I'm not considerate of other people's feelings. I'm not patient. I don't think with my head *and* my heart. I grew up wanting to be like Brady—sorry, Aiden," I say to my other older brother. "You were cool too, but Brady was the one who'd tell me a watermelon wouldn't *actually* grow in my stomach after I swallowed those watermelon seeds. Brady was the one who *didn't* tell Ma that I egged that asshole's car that one time. Anyway…I don't blame you for liking Brady more than me, Hannah. And I'm going to try to be more like him again. For the woman's sake and for mine… I forgot to bring my drink up with me, but here's to recognizing love and to respecting it enough to go after it with your whole heart, even when you aren't drunk."

I go over to hug Brady and Hannah, to shake hands with Hannah's family and everyone at their table. And then I head for the exit because I'm going to try calling Maddie one more time. But I stop in my tracks when I spot the most beautiful woman in the room, and she's staring right at me.

My brain is still a little slower than usual, but my feet start taking me to her immediately.

Or maybe it's my heart that's finally leading me in the right direction.

My head is screwed on straight again.

Oxygenated blood is coursing through my veins again, but most of it's going directly to my cock.

I'm awake and alert and at ease.

Because there she is. The woman I love. She's still wearing her winter coat. Her shiny brown hair is up in a bun, her lower lip is quivering, and her big brown eyes are about to spill over with tears. The woman I've wanted to call and text and see again and again, ever since the first time we spoke. The woman who has handled me exactly the way I've always needed to be handled. The woman I should have said this to on Christmas night: "I love you."

I take that gorgeous face in my hands and kiss her on the mouth. Hard and fast, because I've been dying to do this for so long. And then slow and tender because I know that I'll be kissing this woman every day for the rest of my life. "I love you," I say again between kisses. "I'm so in love with you."

And then I remember that I need to listen to what she came here to say.

"I love you," I say once more. "I'm not going to have the last word—you talk now. Hi."

THIRTY-SEVEN

Maddie

LOVE CRAPTUALLY

I sort of just want to hear Declan Cannavale tell me he's in love with me about a thousand more times before I start talking, but he's looking at me so intently, still holding my face in his hands, so what else can I say to him other than: "I love you too. I heard your speech. I loved what you said. All of it."

"You heard the whole thing?"

"You were just picking up the mic when I walked in."

He keeps staring at my mouth. "Are you hungry? Do you need to eat?"

"I stress ate all morning and at the airport, actually."

He rubs my shoulders and arms through my puffy coat. I really hope he doesn't insist on staying, because I do not want to take my coat off here in front of

Declan's family and a bunch of strangers. "You wanna get out of here?" he mutters.

"Yes. Yes. I do."

"Let's go." He takes my hand and leads me toward the exit.

"Don't you want to tell someone you're leaving?"

"I'll text them from the cab… Shit. The hotel room might be a disaster."

I laugh. "Oh, it was. I went to the hotel first and got the room key, since my name was on the reservation. I called housekeeping to take care of it as soon as I walked in."

"God, I love you. You think of everything. I love everything about you."

"Declan," I say without breaking stride. "I'm still taking another job. I can't work for you when I feel this way."

"I know. It sucks. I'll never find another assistant as good as you. But I understand."

"I will help you find another assistant."

"Damn right you will. *And* train her."

"And train *you.*"

"Good luck with that. But first, please elaborate as to how you feel."

"Madly in love with you."

"Right."

"Deliriously attracted to you."

"Excellent."

Declan gets his coat from the coat check, but I continue talking anyway.

"Unable to keep my hands off you."

"Great to hear."

"Moved beyond words by your generosity and thoughtfulness."

"Well, that's a first."

"I know you got Cindy that karaoke machine. I know you gave my landlady a new coat."

He tries to frown, but he can't stop smiling. "I was just bribing them, you know that."

"Nope. You've got a big heart, Declan Cannavale. And I'm going to tell everyone."

"Then I'll have to sue you for defamation of character."

"I'll tell everyone you watched *Love Actually* with my family and that you cried."

"*Pssh.* I was crying from trying so hard not to laugh at how cheesy it was."

"Nope. You weren't. I'm gonna show you and the world just how sweet you are. Everyone will know you're full of crap every time you try to act like a cocky asshole."

"Okay, that's enough out of you, Coop." He gets me to stop talking in the most wonderful way.

And we don't stop kissing for more than a few seconds, all the way back to the hotel room.

He removes his coat and drops it to the floor as soon as we're inside the door, but I slowly unzip mine, stepping away from him so he can stop and get a good look at the dress I'm wearing. It's a black sleeveless gown with a plunging neckline and a slit that goes all the way to my upper thigh. It's one of the many sale items I've purchased online over the years, just in case

I ever got invited to one of those masquerade balls that people always seem to go to in dirty romance novels.

"Jesus, Mary, and Joseph."

"Piper packed my suitcase for me. She seems to be under the impression that Cleveland is on a very fancy, sexy tropical island. She only threw in sleeveless dresses, four-inch heels, and lingerie. No stockings."

"I really love that kid. When's her birthday? I'm going to buy her a car."

"Wait till you see what's underneath this thing." I lift the straps and let them fall from my shoulders, shimmying out of the dress and then turning around slowly so Declan can get the full picture of me in a scalloped lace bodice teddy and strappy heels.

He slides his hand down the side of his face and says, "I'm going to buy her a house" as he tackles me and we both land on the bed. "How do I get you out of this thing without ripping it apart?"

"There are snaps down there."

"That might be my favorite thing you've said to me so far tonight." He finds the snaps down there. "I just need to tell you one more thing with words, and then I'm going to tell you everything I have ever wanted to say to you with my mouth and my tongue and my fingers and my cock."

"Go on…"

He massages my hips and kisses the inside of my thigh and then says, "I need you to know that I might not always be in a good mood, and sometimes it might seem like I'm more focused on work than anything else. But I will always, always love you more than anything. Okay?"

"Okay. I get you now, Declan. I get you." I interlace my fingers with his.

"Also, I didn't mean it when I said I wouldn't write you a letter of recommendation about your fake girlfriend skills. You were top-notch."

"Well, thank you, but that's the kind of thing you can go ahead and tell me with your mouth and your tongue and your fingers and your cock."

I can feel that mouth smiling against my skin.

"Yes, ma'am. You're the boss of me."

"Yes, sir, I am."

Declan had a lot to say to me with his mouth and tongue and fingers and cock last night. I let him relieve himself of his Catholic guilt all over me, again and again, and forgave him for his very minor sins, again and again. And I smacked him on the butt just once, for Bex and Piper.

We managed to get about five hours of sleep. I was able to buy a pair of stockings from the hotel gift shop and borrow a cardigan from Casey. So, for the wedding I look like a very tired but satisfied high-class prostitute who doesn't want to catch a cold. Declan looks so handsome in his tux; I burst into tears as soon as I saw him. I no longer feel conflicted about whether or not to kiss or slap his gorgeous face when he gets me all riled up. I will always, always kiss him. But I will also always say whatever I have to, to put him in his place.

I already have three meetings scheduled with possible future employers for next week, and according to the recruiter, they are all very eager to hire me and willing to get very competitive with their offers. I will take my time finding the happiest, most polite attorney at the company with the most relaxed work culture possible. Because I only need one moody lawyer in my life, and Declan and I are both going to get serious about that work-life balance thing.

He asked me to move in with him while we were eating breakfast in bed this morning. One step at a time, I told him. I need to get settled at a new job and see how we are together as a couple first. But I already know how we are together, and I love it. I just don't want to break Mrs. Pavlovsky's heart again by moving out too soon. Maybe at the end of February, so Declan and I can take her out for Valentine's Day dinner or something to soften the blow.

The wedding ceremony at the church was long and lovely. The reception and New Year's Eve party is at a different hotel ballroom—all sparkly with black and gold decorations—and we've been dancing for about an hour now. It's getting close to midnight. My date disappeared a couple of minutes ago and left me here on the dance floor with his cousins Nolan and Billy. I honestly don't know if I believe what he told me about them—they're so sweet and polite.

The Motown song segues to "Come and Get Your Love," and I look around for Declan because I need to make fun of him immediately. As I'm craning my neck, I spot him. In that beautiful tux, his dress shirt unbuttoned, bowtie undone and hanging casually around his neck. The crowd between us parts to make way for him because he's doing that ridiculous Star-Lord dance, headed my way. Same as he did that time in the hotel room, except he's not naked. Nolan and Billy do the dance too, moving away from me.

Declan spins around with his arms in the air, and when he reaches me, he drops to one knee. It takes me a few seconds to realize what's happening, because people have formed a big dancing circle around us, and I'm really into this song. But when he reaches into his jacket pocket and holds up a diamond ring, I nearly burst into tears again.

"Maddie Cooper…I want to live with you. I want to marry you. I want to make babies with you. I want to grow old with you. I want you to bury me and cry over my grave, and then I want to fall in love with you all over again in heaven. Or hell. We'll see how good I am at atoning for my sins."

"Wow. That is the most Catholic thing anyone has ever said to me."

"I just spent an hour at a Catholic wedding. What'd you expect? Also, I want to go to Ireland and Italy with you."

"Anything else?"

"Everything, Cooper. Literally, everything else. Will you marry me?"

"Yes. Yes, Declan Sullivan Cannavale, I am going to marry the crap out of you."

I hold my left hand out so he can slide the ring onto my finger. It's a little loose, but it's antique and stunning. Everyone around us, including the bride and groom, are cheering and applauding, and then they go back to dancing to give us some privacy. He stands up to kiss my hand. "Nonna let me borrow her engagement ring until we find the perfect one for you in New York."

I look around for Nonna, who is sitting at a table at the edge of the dance floor. She's frowning at me, but she gives me a thumbs-up. I blow her a kiss, and then I kiss Declan. The song fades out, and somewhere Declan's parents are doing the countdown to midnight into a microphone, but we just keep on kissing into next year.

It's the perfect way to celebrate our new beginning together—as a real couple, drunk in love. Partners who can take turns bossing each other around in and out of the bedroom. I'll be sure to add a clause in our marriage contract that ensures he'll dance naked for me at least once a month for the rest of his life.

Gold confetti is being dumped on us, and people are singing "Auld Lang Syne" by the time we finally pull away long enough to take a breath and say to each other, "Happy New Year, future wife."

"Happy New Year, future husband."

And then we kiss again, for *auld lang syne.*

Whatever that means.

EPILOGUE ONE - Piper

January 1st

Dear Diary,

I can't believe it was only one year ago that Declan's butt came into my life, and now I'm actually related to that butt by marriage. As of yesterday, he is my uncle. So I guess I shouldn't be staring at or thinking about his butt anymore. Or not as much, anyway.

I'm sort of related to Eddie Cannavale by marriage now too, but I Googled it, and we could still legally marry each other. I know I'm only fourteen, and he seems to be really super in love with someone who isn't me and will probably marry her—but I need to know my legal romantic options. Being around Uncle Declan has rubbed off on me LOL.

Anyhoo… The wedding. I think Maddie was a little nervous that Declan and the rest of the guys from the bachelor party wouldn't even make it to the ceremony, but they totally did. Supposedly one of Declan's cousins passed out on the Staten Island Ferry, and another one of them woke up at the zoo, but even they made it on time.

It was definitely the nicest one I've ever been to. Okay it's the only one I've ever been to. But it was even nicer than most of the movie ones I've seen. I guess they are making New Year's Eve weddings a tradition in the Cannavale family or something. Not that the Irish side of their family needs an excuse to get hammered and party all night LOL.

From what I heard, some people in Declan's family were a little miffed that Maddie isn't Catholic, but they had a priest marry them at a really cool space in the West Village, and once everyone saw how pretty it was I don't think anyone cared that it wasn't at a church. Everything was gold and silver and black and white. Mom was matron of honor, of course, and I got to be a bridesmaid! We wore gold dresses, and I was paired up with Eddie!!! As Great Aunt Mel would say—could you die?! So pictures of us might end up on celebrity gossip sites! I keep checking but nothing yet. Oh well I'm totally going to send them some.

Maddie wore a glittering silver and white gown and when Declan saw her walking down the aisle with her dad, he started crying. Not like a big baby, but like a man who is head over heels in love with his stunning wife. It was really cute, and the way they looked at each other…it made me want to grow up.

This beautiful old lady named Mrs. P-something got up and read a Russian poem at the reception and she was all funny and dramatic. And then Mel got up and gave a speech that was also funny and dramatic but in a totally different way. Declan's nonna baked like fourteen different kinds of Italian pastries, and she made me eat all of them. I will probably need a whole new wardrobe because I gained like twenty pounds overnight. None of it went to my boobs though, unfortunately.

The first song that Maclan danced to was "Come and Get

Your Love" and they did the Star-Lord thing together. It was really funny. But also kind of hot. At some point, Declan got up and sang "The Way You Look Tonight" to Maddie. He was kind of drunk and messed up the lyrics, but it was sweet anyway.

I think literally all of the adults in my family are either still drunk, or they are totally hungover. Maddie and Declan left for a couples resort in Antigua. One of his lawyer friends had told him about it. He was at the wedding and whoa! I might have to go into corporate law instead of writing. I wish it wasn't the middle of winter and that the ceremony was at a pool, because I bet that guy has like a ten-pack of abs.

But back to Maclan. I think both of them are really happy that Maddie changed jobs. This way they can be an actual couple and not worry about who's supposed to be the boss in their relationship. Because obviously Maddie is. But Declan is still Boss Butt. Wait I'm not supposed to talk about his butt anymore. Oh well. The assistant that Maddie found for him is an older lady. She was at the wedding, and she reminds me of the principal at my school. She keeps him in line at the office and Maddie keeps him in line at home, that's what my aunt says.

She wrote me a long note in the card along with my bridesmaid gift, thanking me for seeing things with her and Declan even before she was able to. She didn't exactly acknowledge that I'm the reason they got together, but she did say that if I hadn't kept stealing her phone to text Declan, they might not have had as good a time together over the holidays last year as they did. So that's something.

And Declan keeps promising to buy me a car when I get my driver's license, so that's cool too.

Well, I guess I should go check on the baby since you're probably still sleeping, ya big lush.

Yes, I know you're still reading my journal sometimes, Mom. Maybe this year you'll stick to your New Year's resolution of NOT snooping around my room anymore. Love you anyway.

Happy New Year.

EPILOGUE TWO

DECLAN: Babe. You need to come back immediately.
MADDIE: <woman facepalming emoji> Dec. I literally just got in the car. What's wrong?
DECLAN: She won't stop staring at me.
MADDIE: Well, you're her daddy. She probably can't believe how handsome you are. Also, babies can only see things that are 8 to 12 inches from their faces. If you're looking at her in the crib, then you're probably just a big handsome blur to her.
DECLAN: But she's not blinking.
MADDIE: Pretty sure that's normal, babe. Newborns only blink like twice a minute.
DECLAN: Are you sure? What if she's scared of me? I think you should come back.
MADDIE: Babe. I have loved being at home with the two of you all week, but I need to get

out of the house for like half an hour. I'm just going to pop over to see Bex and everyone at her place for a few minutes. You'll both be fine. Just let her go to sleep.
DECLAN: I can't stop staring at her though. She's so beautiful. And I don't want her to think she's alone.
MADDIE: Well, why don't you tell her how you feel? You're so good at that now, remember?
DECLAN: I just told her you guys are the most important people in the world to me, and she rolled her eyes. Wonder where she learned THAT?
DECLAN: Oh wait! She just blinked. She's fine. It's cool.
MADDIE: See?! All is well. I'm gonna start driving now. I'll be back in half an hour. One hour, tops.
DECLAN: Be back in half an hour.
MADDIE: <face with rolling eyes emoji> Bossy!
DECLAN: I think we both know who's the boss in this family now, and she just pooped her pants. And now she's crying. Perhaps you can hear her from the car, because holy shit she is screaming. Please just come back now.
MADDIE: I showed you how to change her diaper, Big Daddy. You got this. Sing Ciara a song and give her a kiss for me. I love you.
DECLAN: I love you, Mrs. Cannavale. Miss you already.

MADDIE: Make sure the baby goes back to sleep. And be naked when I get back.
DECLAN: Yes, ma'am.

Acknowledgments

Thanks to Wildfire Marketing Solutions and Give Me Books for handling my book promotions.

Thanks to Jen Mirabelli for being so supportive, and for conveniently being half-Irish, half-Italian, and for living on Long Island.

Thank you to Lalinc Proofreading for the beta read!

Grazie, Mónica Sablone, for the Italian curse word.

I would like to thank my aunt (who will never ever read my books) for giving me that bottle of merlot a few years ago, because it got me through the sexy scenes, and it tasted pretty good too.

Much love and gratitude to Redbone for "Come and Get Your Love," and to Marvel, Chris Pratt, James Gunn and Star-Lord for one of the best opening credit sequences ever.

If you would like to follow the cover model Stefano Maderna on Instagram (I mean why wouldn't you?), here he is: https://www.instagram.com/stefano_maderna/

So much THANK YOU to @bookaddict_reviews for

finding him and the photographer for me, because the company I bought the image from wouldn't give me any info!

It was grand having Connor Crais and Mackenzie Cartwright's sexy voices in my head while I was writing this, and I can't wait to have them in my ears in December when the audiobook comes out!

As always, I am so grateful to the Bookstagrammers and Facebookers and readers who are so supportive of me and my books. How did I ever live without you?

May you have warm words on a cold evening, a full moon on a dark night, and a smooth road all the way to your door…

Also by Kayley Loring

Eddie Cannavale's story is called A Very Friendly Valentine's Day and it's out now!

Nolan's story will be out before St. Patrick's Day 2022!

All of Kayley Loring's books can be found on Amazon in Kindle Unlimited.

Made in the USA
Las Vegas, NV
21 November 2021